THE ALPHA PLAGUE 8

A POST-APOCALYPTIC ACTION THRILLER

MICHAEL ROBERTSON

EDITED AND COVER BY

Edited by:

Terri King

And

Pauline Nolet

Cover Design by:

Christian Bentulan

Michael Robertson
© 2017 Michael Robertson

The Alpha Plague 8 is a work of fiction. The characters, incidents, situations, and all dialogue are entirely a product of the author's imagination, or are used fictitiously and are not in any way representative of real people, places or things.

Any resemblance to persons living or dead is entirely coincidental.

All rights reserved

No part of this publication may be reproduced, stored in a retrieval system or transmitted in any form or by any means electronic, mechanical, photocopying, recording or otherwise, without the prior written permission of the author except in the case of brief quotations embodied in critical articles and reviews.

MAILING LIST

Would you like to be notified of all my future releases and special offers? Join my spam-free mailing list for all of my updates at www.michaelrobertson.co.uk

CHAPTER 1

They'd walked no more than ten metres from the viewpoint overlooking Home when Flynn's body wound tight. Reluctance pulled on his momentum. A rock balled in his stomach. Sure, he always had that, but this time, it had crawled all the way up into his shoulders and jaw. They'd killed Vicky. Should he be walking away from that without punishing them? A deep breath to try to calm himself, he looked across at Rose. She stared back at him, the wind tossing her long blonde hair.

Just looking at her helped calm him a little, and after he'd tried to release some of the tautness wound within him, he said, "Serj told me anger was like a hot coal."

They continued walking, the swish of the long grass between them. Although Rose watched Flynn, she didn't reply.

"He said no matter who you throw it at, you still get burned." As much as he tried, he couldn't keep the warble from his voice. The thought of killing his friend, as well as the anger about what had happened to Vicky, took nearly everything he had. Heat spread through his cheeks and his eyes itched. Several blinks and he fought back his tears. "I understand what he was saying, but I *can't* forgive them, Rose. No matter how I try to think about it. I mean, I can see why they did what they did. Vicky started this whole mess, after all."

"There is that," Rose said.

"And they're not evil people; I can see that too." Flynn stared down into the valley they were heading into, fighting the urge to turn around and go back towards Home. "I mean, they're not the Queen or Moira. They were acting in what they thought were the community's best interests. But it doesn't take away the pain." The same lump he'd had in his throat for years lifted and Flynn coughed several times to try to clear it. "It doesn't make it any less personal for me."

Rose moved closer to Flynn and put a hand on his back. He wanted to melt against her touch as she spoke, her voice soft. "It'll get easier with time. I'm not sure it'll ever go away, but you need to focus on your pain and heal that. Anger is a secondary emotion, a reaction to the truth. You're sad, and that's okay, but deal with that. Don't be a slave to your rage."

No one had ever said that to him before, not in that way. Serj had probably tried to with his proverbs, but Rose spoke straighter than Serj. It helped. A nod and Flynn bit down on his bottom lip. After another deep inhale, the fresh meadow's air filling his lungs, he said, "Maybe going back to take the Queen down will help. If I protect them by making sure the Queen can't hurt them … I dunno, that compassion might make me feel some kind of forgiveness towards them, right? It might help me care for the people I want to hate."

Rose shrugged and then squinted as she turned to look where they were heading. The setting sun shone in their faces. "Sure." She didn't sound convinced, but they both knew they had to do this. Neither of them could walk away knowing what the Queen had planned.

Before Flynn could respond, he heard a clicking sound from behind. Not quite a snapping stick, more the call of a strange animal. A hard tongue hitting a xylophone tooth. An animal he certainly didn't recognise. He looked back up the hill to see them come over the brow of it. "Fuck!"

Rose then looked behind, her face turning pale, her jaw loose. "Nomads!"

The nomads, although about fifty metres away, had already seen them. Hard not to when they stood in plain sight. What appeared to be the leader of the pack—a large man covered in dirt and dried blood—raised his club. It looked to be the broken-off branch of a tree. It looked to be stained with blood. Stained with use.

Despite the distance separating them, his hiss called over the meadow as if it rang in Flynn's ears. It reverberated around his skull and turned his blood cold. The near animalistic sound came close to paralysing him. So far away from any noise a human would make, he nearly gave himself over there and then.

The rest of the nomads joined in. They hissed like a nest of angry snakes. About twenty of them in total, they burst to life, rushing at Flynn and Rose as a stampede.

Flynn took off and heard Rose follow him. The swoosh of the long grass yielded in front of them. An uneven ground, he led the way over lumps of old road and muddy trenches. Hopefully they wouldn't fall. A broken ankle and they had no chance of escape; even a trip would lose them their advantage.

At the bottom of the hill, Flynn's heart beat treble time. He gulped at the hot evening air and continued up the other side of the valley.

Maybe they could outrun them, maybe not. A look behind and they already seemed to be opening the slightest lead, but they couldn't run forever. And the pack of nomads undoubtedly had people with better endurance than Flynn and Rose.

When he reached the top of the hill, his legs on fire from the climb, Flynn gasped to try to fill what felt like rapidly shrinking lungs. A river with a bridge crossing it ran through the next valley. The only way out of there, he kept going, heading for it with Rose still at his shoulder.

Although Flynn heard the shrieks and cries behind them, a glance showed him they hadn't appeared at the top of the hill yet. The incline had slowed their progress.

Gravity working in his favour, Flynn tried to relax and let his momentum carry him down to the bridge. Once they crossed it, they'd have another expanse of meadow beyond.

A thick tree line on either side of the river would temporarily hide them from view. Maybe they could do something with that.

A few metres before the bridge, Flynn looked behind again to see a red-faced Rose, but not a single nomad.

INSTEAD OF CROSSING THE BRIDGE WHEN HE REACHED IT, Flynn ran down the bank towards the water. Rose followed as he crawled beneath it and nestled into the dark and damp spot where the muddy bank met the wooden sleepers. The reek of wet earth and rot hung heavy in the air. It felt harder to breathe, almost as if the humidity stole the oxygen from their space.

The loud rush of the moving water made it impossible to gauge the nomads' approach. Both Flynn and Rose sat in the darkness, gasping for breath. The coolness of the spot they'd chosen lay against Flynn's bare and sweating arms.

The bandages Rose had wrapped around Flynn's wrists remained. Dirty, his sweat gathered in them and burned his exposed cuts. The ropes had worn deep into his flesh, so the wounds would take some time to heal.

The water ran close to where they sat. Dark with both the fading light and its depth, the current surged through it. It dared Flynn to slip. It would relish the chance to drag him under with the hundreds of corpses that had no doubt already rotted on the riverbed.

So much water in front of them seemed to mock Flynn's dry throat. Not that he could drink any; it probably had the plague running through every thimbleful of it.

In the past, Vicky had saved Flynn when he fell into the river. But he couldn't think about that. They had about half a metre of muddy bank between them and the water. Not a huge amount, but enough.

As Flynn and Rose sat there, shoulder to shoulder, they waited for the nomads. Maybe it hadn't been the best place to hide. Hopefully they wouldn't look for them there. Hopefully they'd be too busy giving chase to stop.

Then Flynn saw it. Just the slightest shift to start with. It could have been his paranoia, but it looked like a small amount of the riverbank crumbled away and fell into the water. Nothing to worry about. If only someone told his quickening heart that.

Then another chunk fell off. He and Rose were too heavy for it. If the bank gave way, they'd be screwed. Knocked unconscious by the weighty sleepers above as the bridge collapsed, they'd drown in the deep river before they came to.

A full inhale and Flynn spoke as quietly as he could, his panic running a staccato through his voice. "Rose."

She looked at him, her mouth wide as she fought for breath, her brow damp with sweat.

"I can't swim. If I fall in ..." Panic stole the rest of his words.

Before Rose could reply, another chunk of the wet earth fell into the river with a splash. They both watched it spin on the surface for a few seconds before the churning water ripped it apart. Then the thunder of the approaching nomads cut through the air.

While listening to the murderous pack approach, Flynn stared down at the dark blue chaos in front of him. They had no other choice but to wait. Wait and pray.

The thud of feet ran onto the bridge above them and Flynn looked up. The thick trees blocked out any light, so he couldn't see through the gaps. Although, over the years, the gaps between the large railway sleepers had mostly clogged with mud anyway.

A train passing over them, the crowd of nomads streamed across the bridge.

Another chunk of riverbank split off and sank into the water. Already pressed against her, Flynn moved even closer to Rose.

When Rose reached out for Flynn's hand, he reciprocated. The mud turned gritty where their fingers linked. As disempowered as he felt to rely on her, at least he knew she would try to save him if something happened and they fell in.

CHAPTER 2

Flynn continued to look up and watch the underside of the bridge. Anything had to be better than the watery death in front of him. The last footsteps had passed over it a few minutes previously and nothing since then. "Do you think they've all gone across?" he said to Rose, his eyes—as much as he tried to fight it—moving down to where the crumbling riverbank met the water.

With a shrug, Rose said, "I don't know. It's impossible to tell." She spoke through a clamped jaw from where the cold of the damp space clearly affected her. They were both still dressed in just T-shirts and joggers. The wet ground had soaked through Flynn's trousers; no doubt the same had happened to her.

"What if some have stayed behind?" Flynn said.

A moment's pause, Rose shrugged again. "I suppose we have to take a chance by emerging at some point."

Although they spoke, they didn't raise the level beyond a whisper. The loud rush of the water in front of them would mask the sound of their voices. Hopefully.

Another chunk of the muddy slope in front of them fell

away into the water and Flynn shook to watch it. He pressed back into the space where the bridge met the bank, hunching over with the pinch of the tight angle. It crushed his body and the smell of damp smothered him as he drew quick, panicky breaths.

It took for Rose to twist her hand before Flynn realised just how tightly he held onto her. "Sorry," he muttered and completely let go, pressing into the damp ground to keep himself pinned in his spot.

But Rose grabbed his hand again and gave it a gentle squeeze as she forced a tight-lipped smile at him.

Still watching the fast-moving water, Flynn said, "I think we should get out of here now."

When Rose didn't reply, he looked across to see her nod at him. Although they'd spoken before, if they were about to move, they needed to communicate without words.

As he shifted to the right, Flynn suddenly froze. The thunder of footsteps returned, slamming down against the other side of the bridge. A rush of people ran onto it and he quickly returned to the cramped space he'd occupied seconds ago.

A deep inhale of the humid reek, Flynn shook his head as he whispered, "Fuck, that was close." He looked up at the underside of the bridge. The nomads reached the middle and stopped.

Flynn tried to quiet his breaths as he listened to the group above. They communicated in a series of hisses and clicks. One of them sounded like they walked in circles, moving with a torturous monotony of stamping steps above them. "Do you think they know we're here?" he whispered.

A shake of her head, Rose looked up at the underside of the bridge too. She then spoke from the side of her mouth. "At least, I hope not."

Maybe they didn't. Maybe they simply gathered on the bridge to plan their next move. Flynn had spoken to Serj about it several times before, and they'd concluded that ascribing human traits to the nomads didn't make much sense. To try to judge their intentions based on normal human behaviour seemed like a waste of time. They were animals and needed to be viewed as such.

A twist of his wrists to try to ease the burn in them, a shuffle in the mud to relieve the aches in his body, a deep breath into his tight lungs; although Flynn did all of those things, his panic still threatened to drag him under. They might have to fight. He just needed to make sure he hadn't beaten himself in his head before that happened.

A series of whistles and peeps then sounded above them. Moments later, the rush of nomads took flight, moving off the bridge as a pack, back towards Home.

"Maybe they're giving up on us?" Flynn said.

Rose shrugged.

They needed to wait to be sure.

MORE OF THE BANK FELL INTO THE WATER AND FLYNN pressed his feet so deep into the soggy earth his toes ached. God knew how long had passed. It felt like hours. "I think it's been long enough," he said as he watched the dark river in front of them. Breathless from his pulse racing, he added, "I think we should try to get out of here again."

Rose shivered from the cold and nodded.

They both crawled out from a side of the bridge each. Flynn on the right, Rose on the left.

Cautious in his movement, Flynn poked his head up and looked around for nomads. The fading light and shadows created by the trees made it hard to be sure, but it looked clear. He couldn't be any more certain than that.

As Flynn and Rose emerged and climbed up onto the bridge, they both scanned their surroundings.

After a few seconds, Flynn released a long sigh. He reached out and held Rose's hand again, their palms covered in the damp earth from beneath the bridge. "That was close."

Rose shook her head. "It ain't over yet."

"No, you're right." Flynn led the way off the bridge in the opposite direction to where the nomads had just gone. Hopefully they'd given up trying to find them, but like Rose said; it ain't over yet.

CHAPTER 3

They'd been under the bridge long enough for it to be much darker by the time they stepped out of the cover of the trees lining the river. Flynn could still see across the meadow in front of them, but just; much longer and that would be taken away from them too.

The wreck of the old town dominated the skyline as it always did. Although the years had eaten away at it, the skeleton of a previous capitalist existence remained. Not that they'd go anywhere near the place at night. The rats might have behaved themselves during the day, but at night all bets were off. The stories Flynn had heard … a shudder snapped through him.

"I suppose we need to head in the direction of the royal complex until we find somewhere good to rest for the night," Rose said.

Flynn shook his head. "I wonder if we should stay away from there until we've got our energy up. If we get close and see her guards heading for the city where they have the games, we'll have to follow them. We need to free the prisoners so we have an army to march on the Queen with. I'd rather not be presented with that opportunity until I feel rested enough to take it."

A response of sorts, Rose nodded at Flynn's words. They'd already agreed on their course of action. It made sense to mobilise a force against the Queen, and the prisoners seemed like the perfect candidates to be a part of that force.

The stress of their time beneath the bridge with the crumbling riverbank had given Flynn pains in his chest. He drew a deep breath in an attempt to ease the tight twist in his upper body, but it did little to relieve it. "How will we persuade the Queen's prisoners to join us in attacking her? What if they just want to run?"

"I don't know," Rose said. "I wouldn't blame them if they did. I suppose we should cross that bridge when we come to it."

Before Flynn could reply, a shrill and tongue-rolling call rang out over the meadow. The sound of it turned his blood cold and gooseflesh ran up his arms. When he looked to his left in the direction of the noise, he saw them. About ten in total, they ran straight at them. "Nomads!" he called out, and took off at a sprint.

As they ran, Flynn looked behind at the pack giving chase. He then saw the others burst from the tree line they'd just come through and join their friends. The pack had reformed. About twenty in total. So much for losing them.

Only slightly quicker than Rose, Flynn had to make a choice. They were heading in the direction of the abandoned town. The rats would be out in force. Anyone in the town at night would be fair game. It meant it would be as dangerous for the nomads as it would for Flynn and Rose. And the nomads would draw much more attention to themselves. Not a good option, but maybe the best they had.

The nomads had spread out behind them. A wide line,

they hunted as a pack. Soon it would be too dark to keep running. They might have been faster than the nomads, but they had no chance against them at night over uneven ground.

Flynn's feet twisted and turned with almost every step. Even when they could see, it would just be a matter of time before one of them fell.

Fighting for breath, Flynn's wrists were on fire as his sweat ran into his wounds. He focused on the town to take his mind off it and the tattoo of footsteps behind.

The old road into town remained littered with the shells of abandoned vehicles. In the rapidly fading light, it gave them a path to follow, so Flynn headed for it. Still possible to trip, but because it had once had an asphalt surface, it would be a better route than the lumpy earth they currently ran over.

Flynn checked behind again. Rose remained at his shoulder, letting him lead the way. The nomads were falling back slightly.

Maybe the amount of times Flynn had visited the town in the past worked in his favour. As the phallic wreck of the dominant office block got closer, he grew in confidence. He found his rhythm with his breaths and pushed on. When they got into the built-up area, they could hide … if the rats let them, that is.

CHAPTER 4

The slap of Flynn's and Rose's feet echoed beneath the old railway bridge as they entered the town. It amplified the sound of their breathing and gave the pursuing nomads something to chase.

Although Flynn ached with the effort of the run—his lungs ready to burst, his legs weak with every step—he pushed on. A glance back and he couldn't see the nomads. They were on their tail still, but maybe they could give them the slip now they'd entered the rats' domain.

The first building they came to—the one Vicky always referred to when she talked about the diseased chasing her—seemed like the best place to enter. Flynn ran straight for it and jumped through the space where a window had been on the ground floor.

The darkness of the office block bordered on complete, night having well and truly settled in outside. But Flynn quickly adjusted to the poor visibility, and weaved through the downed office chairs and cracked desks as if he knew the place intimately. Something about being chased had heightened his senses.

The building stank of dust and rot, and Flynn inhaled the reek of decomposition all around him, but he pushed forward, dragging the stagnant air into his flagging body.

The sound of Rose followed him, but he dared not turn around. To take his eyes from his path would undoubtedly make him fall over something. As long as he could hear her, he didn't need to worry. She was more than capable of looking after herself. If he gave her something to follow, they'd get through this.

When Flynn hit the double doors at the end of the ground floor, he knocked one open wide and the other one clean off its hinges, sending it clattering against the stairs on the other side before it fell to the ground with a slap. As he continued running, he heard the nomads enter the town behind them, their thunderous stampede amplified by the railway bridge as they charged beneath it.

Instead of hiding in the first building, Flynn ran straight out of the office block into the one next door. Again, Rose followed his mazy path as he zigzagged through the wreck of a life now twenty years forgotten. Serj had called it a cubicle existence. It looked like it had been even more depressing than a world inhabited by the diseased.

After he'd run through the scattering of broken desks, chairs, and computers, Flynn reached a hole where a window had been and vaulted through the space.

He charged straight into an old restaurant next door, Rose following him every step of the way.

There were more tables scattered through the restaurant than there had been desks in the offices. Flynn twisted and turned through the much tighter path, his sharp changes of direction threatening his weak legs.

But he reached the doors on the other side of the abandoned eatery and burst through them into the street beyond.

He stumbled, but just managed to keep his balance. A second later, Rose ran out behind him.

Flynn crossed what used to be a road and entered the old pedestrianised area in the high street. The sound of the nomads had died down—maybe they were all searching the first building; maybe they moved soundlessly and were right on their tail. Regardless, they needed to find somewhere to hide. They couldn't run forever.

At the same pace he'd moved at since the nomads had given chase, Flynn headed for the old Wilkinson's shop. The largest building on the high street, it had to be the best place to hide.

Out of breath and sweating, his wrist wounds throbbing with the salty sting of his perspiration, Flynn entered the huge building with Rose still close behind.

The pair of them ran through the old, empty shelves, the shop picked clean from years of scavenging.

When Flynn got to the darkness of the storeroom at the back, he ran in and found a shadowy corner. Rose caught up to him and they huddled together, both fighting to get their breath under control as they crouched down.

Shoulder to shoulder, Flynn and Rose listened for the sounds of the nomads out in the high street.

It took a few seconds before Rose said, "Do you think we've lost them?"

Flynn fought to catch his breath. "I hope so."

CHAPTER 5

God knew how long had passed. Long enough for Flynn to recover his breath and for his tired limbs to turn to lead. If he needed to run again, he might not have it in him.

Although she crouched next to him, still shoulder to shoulder, Flynn couldn't see Rose as anything more than a silhouette because of the darkness. The heat of the run had left him, and the coolness of the evening lay against his sweating skin. It helped to have the warm press of her body next to his.

A constant angry buzz ran through the cuts on Flynn's wrists. They hurt without any stimulation, but after sweating into them all day, they burned as if he had red ants between the bandages and his wounds. The rags were so filthy they probably did more harm than good, but it wouldn't do to take them off now; he couldn't care for what he couldn't see. They'd have to re-dress them in the morning.

Although not total darkness in the storeroom, Flynn could only see his surroundings as blocky shadows. Shelves, tables, and upturned boxes all existed as shapes and nothing more.

The only light came from the doorway leading to the shop, where the weak moon shone in through the front.

Just as Flynn drew a breath to speak, the sound of people outside took the words from his mouth. He felt Rose snap rigid next to him and jumped at her sharp movement. "Shit," he whispered, "I thought we'd lost them." He knew it to be the nomads because a series of clicks and whistles ran through the night instead of voices. They could speak, he'd heard them speak, but it would seem they went more basic than that when on the hunt.

"Are they in the shop?" Rose whispered back.

"I don't know." Flynn shook as his fatigue mixed with fear-driven adrenaline. "It doesn't sound like it. Maybe we'll be okay if we stay here. They can't search everywhere, right?"

But Rose didn't reply. Instead, she snapped her head in a different direction and pushed against Flynn as if trying to shift away from something, something in the room with them.

When Flynn looked around the storeroom, he couldn't see what it could be, and then the shadowed area around them moved. A large part of what he'd perceived as abandoned furniture shifted, closing in on them.

A pair of eyes opened and stood out from the darkness. Just one person at first. Then more around it glowed into existence.

The small crowd of little people shifted forwards again. Maybe ten, maybe more, they were a pack ready to pounce.

Flynn stared at the closest rat, and the rat stared at him. The army behind it clearly stood ready to follow its lead.

CHAPTER 6

The clicks and whistles of the nomads in the high street grew louder. The heads of the rats turned in the direction of the sound before they snapped back to look at Flynn and Rose. They moved as if of the same mind.

The shadows shuffled in front of them again and more rats stepped forward. More pairs of eyes popped from the darkness. More pairs of feet scraped over the dusty ground. Even with the poor visibility, Flynn saw the hunger in their haunted and hollow stares.

If Flynn had to pick a fight against one of the groups, it would have to be the rats. Maybe he could lunge at the leader and cave its little skull in. An act of brutality that would make the others back off. Or would it enrage them and make the pack swarm him and Rose? Either way, whichever group they fought, they'd be lucky to walk away afterwards.

Maybe if Flynn made enough noise, he could draw the nomads in and make them and the rats fight. Both groups would present a larger threat to one another than he and Rose would to either.

Before Flynn could do anything, Rose pushed harder

against him as if spooked by something else. When he listened, he heard the sound of people entering the shop.

The rats seemed to hear it at the same time. The blinking and hungry eyes all turned in the same direction again, looking through the doorway towards the noise. It clearly rattled them. As one they withdrew into the shadows, closing their eyes as they melted back into the darkness.

Flynn shifted forward and peered through the storeroom's doorway into the shop. Nearly as little visibility outside the storeroom as in it, the front windows let in the smallest amount of moonlight. It allowed him to see a little more clearly.

Not that Flynn needed to see to track the nomads. They moved like bears ransacking bins. Crashes and bangs as they worked their way through the abandoned space, they turned over furniture and shoved obstructions aside. As long as they stayed in the shop and didn't head for the storeroom, everything would be fine.

Wishful thinking.

Tension wound through Flynn as the sounds drew closer to them. He moved back until he pressed against Rose again. For a short time, he listened to her quickened breaths before he said, "We might need to fight them. If we can take the few out who have come into the shop, it'll reduce the overall numbers. If they've all split up, we might end up facing small groups of three or four at a time. We can beat that."

Although Rose didn't reply, Flynn felt her nodding.

The sound of the nomads drew closer and Flynn clenched his fists, his wrists buzzing. He stepped forward again and peered through the doorway.

Flynn froze as he watched the silhouettes of four adults. What little energy he thought he had drained from his body.

No way would he and Rose take them down in their current state. Even four would be too many.

The silhouettes continued to turn shelves and furniture over, and they continued to make their way towards the storeroom.

But they'd have to try to fight them. They couldn't do anything else. A deep breath to settle his pulse, Flynn studied the silhouettes. It looked like four men, but he couldn't be certain. Regardless, they'd beat him and Rose in a fight.

The four nomads drew closer until they were just a few metres away. But then a whistle rang through the shop from outside. They halted and all turned to face the direction of the sound. One of them whistled back. Another whistle responded. As one, the four nomads took off and ran back towards the high street.

After he'd listened to them run out of the shop, Flynn looked at where the rats had been. He couldn't see anything.

"Do you think they've all gone?" Rose said.

A shrug at her, Flynn said, "I hope so. I'm not sure I've got a fight in me if they haven't."

CHAPTER 7

At least half an hour had passed since they'd seen or heard anything. As much as Flynn appreciated the warm press of Rose's body against his, he said, "I think we should make a move."

Although Rose didn't speak, he again felt her nod in agreement with him.

The darkness of the storeroom equipped Flynn well for dealing with the abandoned store beyond. Still dark, the open front of the shop where the windows had previously been let in enough moonlight to help them navigate the overturned shelves and discarded furniture.

They walked a slow path. It felt like the crunch of their feet over the dirty ground was the only sound in the entire town. Hopefully neither the nomads nor the rats had set a trap for them. He hoped even more that the nomads had left.

Now he'd pulled away from Rose and her body heat, Flynn shivered. In just a T-shirt and joggers—his bottom still damp from where they'd sat beneath the bridge—the cold of the night bit into him. His wrists burned worse than ever and he could feel the infection spreading through them. Tendrils of pain ran up his forearms as if poison coursed through his veins.

The occasional pop of breaking glass added to their slow exit from the shop. When either one of them stepped on the shards, they'd freeze and listen for sounds outside. Most people wouldn't have heard it, but the rats and the nomads weren't most people. Their animal instincts meant they could probably hear a mouse sigh from the other side of town. If they were close by, they'd definitely heard it.

After he'd checked up and down the high street, Flynn stepped out into the pedestrianised area. Now they were outside, the wind chill ran gooseflesh up his arms and he hugged himself for warmth. A look at Rose and he saw her struggling too, shivering as she clamped her jaw tight.

The moon's silver highlight ran along the tops of old benches and dustbins. It caught the fronts of the decrepit shops and lit up no more than a metre into each building. Flynn shrugged, "I can't see anything, can you?"

"I think that's the problem, isn't it?" Rose said.

Her words sent a spike of adrenaline through Flynn's guts and he stared into the inky void of each shop. Of course she was right; being able to see just the front of each building shouldn't give him any confidence. For all he knew, the rats could be waiting inside every one of them, their hungry little eyes watching them as they decided when to attack.

"Well, I reckon the nomads have gone at least," Flynn said while holding his left wrist with his right hand. "I can't see them staying on the rats' turf for this long."

Rose frowned down at Flynn's grip. "Are your wrists hurting?"

As much as he wanted to say no, Flynn nodded. "Yeah, I'm worried they're infected."

"We need to re-dress them," Rose said.

"We need to get out of this cursed town first." Flynn looked over to the large wall with the fire escape zigzagging down the side of it. It forced an involuntary sigh from him.

"What's up?"

"Remember I told you about Serj?"

"Yeah."

To look at the wall brought back the pain of killing his friend, and Flynn had to compose himself before he spoke. "Well, this is where he died. This is where I killed him."

Rose didn't reply, waiting for him to continue.

"We were out fetching lead for Home. Serj decided to climb up that fire escape over there." He pointed. "When he got to the top, he found the lead wrapped around the bottom of a chimney, stepped onto the roof to get to it, and fell through. He landed on a scaffolding pole three storeys below. It went straight through his stomach."

A sharp intake of breath through her clenched teeth, Rose shook her head. "I'm sorry, Flynn."

"You can probably see why there was no saving him."

Flynn flinched when Rose touched his arm. "And that's why you had to help him pass on. He asked you to do it for a good reason."

Reliving it lifted a burning lump into Flynn's throat and he could only nod in response. "If I didn't kill him, the rats would have eaten him alive. The best I could do was leave a corpse for them rather than make Serj experience that."

"They *ate* him?"

"It's what they do. It's what a lot of people do in this world now. Why let a good meal go to waste?"

"But they're *so* young."

"It's sad, isn't it? So young and so feral."

"Where are the adults?"

A stronger breeze ran up the high street and Flynn shivered again. He scanned their surroundings once more, searching the dark shadows for signs of movement. Although he saw nothing, he still lowered his voice. "We think there are adults in this town. We think they tell them what to do and make them work for them."

"That's awful. Poor kids."

"I know."

"We have to help them."

"How did I know that was coming?" After he looked at Rose and her blank expression, Flynn looked at their surroundings again and shook his head. "No."

"What do you mean *no*?"

"I don't know how you think we can help them, but I'm *not* getting involved. You saw them in the storeroom; they're vicious little fuckers. Give them half a chance and they'll take us down. It'd be suicide getting too close to them."

"They're only vicious because they've been conditioned to be like that. They're *kids*, Flynn. They're children being exploited by adults for their own ends. They should be the personification of hope, but they're little animals instead. It's hardly surprising they're fucked up. Look at the world they're being raised in."

A deep sigh, but Rose cut Flynn off before he could reply.

"God knows what else is happening to them. We *have* to help them. We have to do the right thing by them."

Flynn opened his mouth to object, but Rose cut him off again. "My mum told me to be the change I wanted to see in the world. If her death has any worth, it's for me to honour that wish. I don't want to live in a world where child abuse is accepted and ignored. I *won't* be a part of that. There are so few people left now and we need to make sure our actions count for something; otherwise we might as well give up and let our species die out."

Flynn shook his head. Why had he led them into the town? He should have run straight past it and let them take their chances against the nomads.

CHAPTER 8

Flynn stared at Rose and listened to the sound of the wind running through the town. What could he say to dissuade her from trying to rescue the rats? Sure, he got where she came from, and it was sad to see children subjected to such abuses, but what could they do? How could they communicate their intentions to kids who couldn't understand them? Scared and dangerous kids who probably didn't feel like they needed rescuing anyway.

Flynn finally said, "So what do we do with them afterwards?"

Rose frowned at him. "What do you mean?"

Another look around, the darkness inside every shop staring back at him, Flynn said, "Well, we're going to have a shitload of liberated children, which is great, if they want to be freed."

"*If?*"

"They might think they're doing all right as they are. So let's assume they do want to be freed, what then? We can't look after them. We can't take them with us or feed them."

After a moment's pause, Rose said, "I think we should at least find out what they're about."

"What, find out who runs this town?" Flynn said it as quietly as he could. The rats might not speak, but they could hear. No way of knowing if they understood them or not.

"We have to give it a go."

"No, we don't." A step towards Rose and Flynn lowered his voice again. "I'd be very surprised if they've not listened to this conversation. They've probably heard every word we've said to one another already."

Rose's brown eyes widened slightly and she bit down on her bottom lip as if to hold her words back. She then let go of a deflated sigh and nodded. "Fine! You're right, there's nothing we can do for this lot anyway. Come on, let's get out of here."

Finally, she saw sense. Flynn nodded at Rose, but she only returned a scowl. Better for her to be pissed with him than they get eaten alive by the rats. He moved off towards the town's exit. The sooner they got away from the place, the better.

CHAPTER 9

They didn't speak as Flynn led Rose from the town. The scuff of their feet called through the abandoned spaces, and the wind ran through the deserted shops. Better they walked in silence so they could keep their wits. Besides, the crumbling walls in the place had ears. They needed to get out of there and work out what to do next when they weren't being observed.

Dark shadows sat inside every shop they passed. It made it impossible to assess the depth of each building. It didn't matter how hard Flynn squinted, he had no idea if the small beings lurked inside them or not, and, if they did, how far away they were. At times it looked like the shadows shifted, his heart kicking in response to what he thought he saw, but nothing had come of it yet. So tired at that moment, the line between reality and his imagination blurred.

They passed the restaurant they'd run through earlier and the shuffle of movement called from the windowless building. Flynn's pulse spiked to hear it and he drew in a sharp breath. But he couldn't see the source of the sound. Probably just an animal.

Who was he kidding? In all likelihood, a rat lurked in the darkness, stilling its giddy breath as it watched them through its hollow and haunted eyes. They were everywhere, hanging back just out of sight, deciding if they should let Flynn and Rose leave the town. A shudder snapped through him. He shook his head to himself; they could only deal with what got placed in front of them. At present, they had nothing other than architectural ruin. He couldn't be afraid of the shadows.

When they passed the large derelict office building they always saw upon entering the town in the past, Flynn looked up at the top floor. Vicky had told him about how she and Hugh were chased into it and all the way up by the diseased, and how they had swung down over the edge to jump onto the floor below. It must have been something to see.

The diseased seemed like a lifetime ago now. It had been years since Flynn had heard the deranged scream that used to send ice down his spine. Who'd have thought he'd get to a point where a pack of children became a more tangible threat than a mob of diseased?

They passed under the railway bridge—the scuff of their feet amplified by the enclosed space—and stepped out into the meadow beyond. A shiver ran through Flynn to get hit by the strong wind in the open space. He hugged himself for warmth, his movements so clumsy he banged his sore wrists together. The connection sent a buzzing shock streaking up his forearms, making him realize the sooner he changed the bandages, the better.

No buildings to block the wind, Flynn stumbled as he walked and looked around the dark plains. Night had well and truly settled in now they'd left the town. A look at Rose and his eyes dropped to her breasts. No bra beneath her thin T-shirt left little to his imagination.

He quickly looked away. No one wanted to be that guy. Heat flushed his cheeks just to think of her catching him. She was so much more than a hot physique. Besides, if he judged her current body language correctly, she seemed ready to swing for him.

"We need to find somewhere to settle for the night," Flynn said.

Rose didn't reply and turned her head away from him as he spoke, her jaw clenched.

"Okay …" Flynn said. But even then, Rose still didn't respond.

The long grass dragged against Flynn's thighs and waist as he walked. The cold night had dampened the blades, which quickly soaked through his trousers.

Other than the sound of the wind and the swish of the long grass, Flynn heard nothing. The nomads weren't known for going out at night.

Because he'd walked to the town and back countless times, Flynn knew exactly where to go. A look across the meadow and he saw the large silhouette of it like he'd done many times before.

From what Flynn had been able to tell over the years, the barn had been abandoned a long time ago and served no purpose for anyone. Not that he could take it for granted, but it seemed like a good starting point.

When Flynn stopped, Rose looked at him. He pointed across the meadow. "I think we should stay in there tonight."

The wind blew through Rose's hair as she looked to where he pointed, her jaw set. She didn't respond any more than with a flick of her head.

"Are you going to ignore me for the rest of the night?"

Rose still said nothing.

∼

It took them about ten minutes to get to the barn. Neither of them spoke for the rest of the walk, and by the time Flynn got there, his trousers, underpants, boots, and socks were soaked from the wet grass. Every step returned a cold squelch.

If there had been a door on the large wooden barn in the past, Flynn saw no trace of it now. A look into the place as they approached it and it seemed clear. The roof somehow remained on it, although the entire structure looked ready to collapse. He continued in.

Because the entrance stretched so wide, it let in the moonlight, which shone through most of the building. It looked completely abandoned like Flynn had expected it to be. Rotten wood and dust made it smell like no one else had been in there for a long time.

There were so few people left now, it would have been bad luck to come across another group of squatters. If you weren't a nomad or a member of a community, then you were dead. In all the years Flynn had been in Home for, he hadn't seen any trace of nomads in or around the barn.

"One dark corner seems as good as any," Flynn said as he headed for the farthest corner from the entrance. But when he turned around, he saw Rose had halted in the doorway. He stopped too. "What are you doing?"

The way Rose shook her head made Flynn fall limp. "I wanted to make sure you found somewhere safe."

"*I* found somewhere safe?"

"I'm going back into the town to free the rats. I said it in the town, and I'll say it again now; I refuse to live in a world that turns their back on abused children. I can't force anyone else to live by those standards, but I can stay true to them myself."

Before Flynn could reply, Rose turned around and walked out of the barn. "I'll be back when I'm done."

CHAPTER 10

Fuck Rose. Let her go and get herself killed in the town. If she didn't want to listen to Flynn, he couldn't do anything to help her. Fuck her.

Grime and dirt covered the barn's concrete ground. It crunched beneath Flynn's steps as he walked across it. He found the darkest corner and eased himself down.

The concrete felt cold to sit on and had zero give. Miserable, cold, and uncomfortable, Flynn sat and stared out through the barn's large doorway. What else could he do? Rose had made it clear she didn't want a discussion about it, and he'd made it clear he didn't want to help the rats.

The fact that Rose had only just walked through the large doorway made it seem emptier than it would have been had she never been there. A stark reminder that she'd left him on his own and, in all likelihood, wouldn't be returning. In that moment, she'd become just a memory, a whisper on the wind. But if she wouldn't listen to him, what could he do?

When Flynn leaned against the wooden wall behind him, it stood firm. Like the ground, it offered little comfort. He wouldn't be sleeping that night. He shifted to try to sit more at ease, but aggravated the brand on his lower back instead. The wound, although better than it had been, hadn't yet healed.

Cold in just his T-shirt, his wrists stinging more than ever, and surrounded by an encroaching darkness, Flynn refused to get up. Fuck Rose. She'd made the choice and she needed to stand by it. It wasn't his place to rescue her.

… even though she'd rescued him by giving up her chance to get away from the games …

Maybe he should follow her. He didn't have to talk to her, but at least he could walk beside her and make sure she didn't kill herself. This world had very few good eggs left in it. It would be a shame to let one crack.

If Flynn waited much longer to run after Rose, he'd completely lose sight of her in the darkness. She'd vanish into the long grass and then the town. She'd be on her own in that hideous place. "Fuck it," he muttered to himself and got to his feet. If nothing else, he needed someone to help him bind his wrists so he could keep them free from infection.

A dark night with the weak moon in the sky, but much lighter outside the barn than in it, Flynn stepped out into the meadow. He saw Rose a good thirty to fifty metres away from him. He'd been correct to get out and after her at that point. Much longer and she would have vanished from his line of sight like he'd thought.

Even raising his hands to cup them around the sides of his mouth sent an angry buzz through his wrists. He drew a deep breath to call out to her and then heard a rustle to his right. It cut him dead, stopping the words before he could yell them. He looked in the direction of the sound.

They looked like nomads, but he could only see two of

them. They followed Rose, spears raised. Rose seemed oblivious. So determined to get to the town, she'd neglected to keep an eye on her surroundings.

CHAPTER 11

No weapons other than his fists, Flynn clenched them, doing his best to ignore the buzz in his wrists. He shouted, "Rose!"

The sound of his call rang out across the meadow. He didn't look to see if Rose had turned around. Not now the two hunters were facing him.

Flynn charged straight at the two spear-wielders, screaming as he ran.

A man and a woman, they both raised their weapons and hunched down, widening their stance. The man panicked and threw his spear too soon. It fell short, planting in the ground like a flag.

The woman had more composure, watching Flynn with her spear raised.

Although he focused on the hunters, the long grass whipping at his stomach and thighs, Flynn saw Rose in his peripheral vision. She charged at them like he did, closing them down from another side.

Then the hunters noticed Rose. They looked between her

and Flynn. Their frames slumped. They'd suddenly lost the advantage and they knew it.

Flynn grabbed the spear the man had thrown at him without breaking stride. While winding it back, he watched the two hunters pull close to one another as if the proximity to one another meant safety. They'd just given him a larger target to hit.

Only a few metres between Flynn and them, the woman then threw her spear. A good shot, but not good enough. It passed Flynn with a *whoosh.* Weaponless, they were now fucked.

Like a pair of spooked animals, they pulled in even tighter to one another. The predators had become prey. Then the man broke away, charging at Flynn with his fists raised.

Flynn turned the spear he'd retrieved into a lance. He held it with both hands and kept running.

The man continued towards him without slowing. A game of chicken only one of them would win.

Flynn drove the spear into the centre of the man's face. A violent kick ran through the wooden pole as the tip of the spear sank into the man's nose. It turned him instantly limp. When he fell, he pulled the weapon with him, snapping its wooden shaft.

Now a club, the broken handle remained about half a metre long. As Flynn ran at the woman, he raised the baton above his head, ready to swing for her. Not that he'd need to attack her. He saw it before she did.

Rose rugby tackled the woman from the side and knocked her to the ground. The loud, "Oomph," she forced from the woman's body sounded like it had driven the air from her lungs.

Breathless or not, the woman couldn't defend herself against Rose's speed. After snatching the spear handle from

Flynn's grip, Rose laid into the woman with repeated blows against the top of her head. They sounded out as hollow *tonks* that quickly gave way with a crunch and then a squelch that turned Flynn's stomach.

Despite the woman clearly becoming no more than a corpse, Rose clenched her teeth and drove several more blows to her pulped cranium. Something sprayed away from the woman. Too dark to see exactly what.

Still riding the rage of her attack, her shoulders raised, her breaths heavy, Rose got to her feet and stared at Flynn. She held the snapped handle like she'd use it against him. "I had to do that." She pointed the bloody baton at the downed woman and spoke through gritted teeth. "I want to help people in this world, but when they come at me like those two just did, there's no helping them." Tears glazed her eyes. "I need to be the change I want to see. I want a world without arseholes like *that* in it."

Reluctant to speak in case he said the wrong thing, Flynn simply nodded at her.

The rage then visibly cleared as Rose relaxed, her arm and the baton falling down to her side. She then let the weapon drop to the ground. A moment later, she spun on her heel and resumed her march towards the town.

CHAPTER 12

Flynn had to jog through the long grass to catch up with Rose. He fell into stride with her, but remained far enough away just in case she swung for him. Not that he'd done much wrong other than save her. Although, maybe that was enough. To look at her tense frame—her shoulders still pulled into her neck and her fierce scowl—should have been enough of a warning to keep his mouth shut. Yet he still said, "See?"

Fire burned in Rose's eyes as she spun on him. "See *what*?" Although shorter and slimmer than Flynn, at that moment she'd knock his head off given half a chance.

Too late to back down, Flynn moved another pace away from her as they walked. "It's *dangerous* out here. And we haven't even reached the town yet. That's why I think we should move on. You agreed with me when we were in there. What's changed?"

"I only said that because *you* said we were being watched. What other options did I have? I didn't want the people in the town to think I was going to return. I would have headed straight back in when we left the place, but I figured I needed to give it a little time so they lowered their guard."

Before Flynn could respond, Rose said, "And those people following me has nothing to do with me going back to help the kids. That could happen at any time in this world."

"But at least you wouldn't have been out in the field in plain sight if you'd have stayed in the barn with me."

Rose stopped for a second, her hands on her hips. "No, I would have been trying to go to sleep on the cold, dusty, concrete ground. I probably would have been ripe for those two hunters to come in and slit my throat while I had my eyes closed. What point are you trying to make, Flynn?"

When Rose set off again, Flynn walked with her. This time he kept his mouth shut.

The large decrepit office building stood on the horizon. Flynn had to shake the thought of Vicky from his mind at that moment. Hard enough to think about her when he felt positive. He broke the silence between them. "Why don't we just move on? We have our own shit to deal with. We won't be any good to Home and the people in the royal complex if we get killed by the rats."

"We won't get killed."

"Now there's a solid plan. Why didn't I think of that?"

Rose sighed and shook her head. "Look, I understand this situation is stressful, but I need to be the change. I can't let kids be abused and taken advantage of. How many times do I have to say it?" After turning around and pointing in the direction of the two hunters they'd just taken down, she said, "There are people like *that* in this world. Who's going to look out for the kids if I don't?"

Silence.

"I'm not asking you to come with me, Flynn."

And she wasn't. "But I can't not," Flynn said, the words leaving his mouth before he'd thought about them.

"Sure you can. Go back to the barn and wait for me."

The rage had clearly left her because she walked more at ease than before. Flynn stepped closer to her and softened his tone. "I can't let you go back in there on your own." His pulse quickened and his lungs tightened at the thought of saying it, of laying himself bare so soon after Angelica. But they'd talked in circles until then, each one being pissed off with the other. Someone had to break the pattern. Heat rushed through his cheeks when he said, "I'm sorry about being a dick. I shouldn't have suggested the hunters attacking us was your fault. The truth is, I don't want to be separated from you. I don't want to sit awake in the barn all night, worrying about you not coming back."

The sounds of the night replied to him: the hoot of an owl, the wind running over the meadow outside, the chirp of crickets. Rose stared at him. She looked like she wanted to say something.

Before she could speak, Flynn shook his head, "Anyway, what do we do when we save the kids? I don't want to look after them."

"You think they need looking after? I thought they got the food and did the hunting? By the sound of it, they'll work it out pretty quickly, I'm sure. Look, I don't want to spend the rest of the night debating it. I'm going back there. You can come if you like, it's your call. Either way, make a choice and accept it."

His face still burning from the shame of Rose's rejection, Flynn kept stride with her and focused his attention on the ruined town. At least he had an answer. She wasn't into him in that way. He'd been a fool to think otherwise.

CHAPTER 13

Rose's rejection of Flynn trebled the weight of the tiredness in his body. Although he continued to follow her, he walked a few steps behind. Cold, exhausted, and with his wrists throbbing with the spread of infection, he felt like going back to the barn. But he couldn't leave her on her own. Rejection or not, he needed to put his ego to one side and do the right thing by her.

The sound of the wind and the swish of the long grass filled what would have been silence between them. Flynn's jaw ached from clenching it tightly against the bitter chill running over the meadow.

The craggy silhouette of the old office block grew in size until it dominated the view. Impossible to look at it and not think of Vicky, regardless of how he tried to shut her out. Flynn looked at the top floor and he heard the call of the diseased ring through his mind. It didn't matter how many years it had been, he could remember the hellish sound like he'd only just heard it.

Several glances over his shoulder, Flynn saw the dark rise of the slope behind them. He saw the large blocky shadows of corroded vehicles on the road. Other than that, it looked clear. If there were any more hunters about, maybe they'd seen what had happened to the last two and thought better of it.

"I've lost a lot of people in this life, Flynn," Rose said.

A frown so deep it dimmed his view of her, Flynn shrugged. "That doesn't make you special."

"*Wow!*"

"Well, what's your point?" Flynn asked, shocked at his own bitterness.

All the while she spoke, Rose stared at the ruined town in front of her. The wind tossed her hair, pulling it back to reveal her beauty beneath. It taunted him. He'd been an idiot to think the feelings would be mutual. "I dunno, I just find it hard to get close to people now."

"I've already got the message, Rose. Let's not dwell on it, yeah? I understand a hint, you don't need to fucking spell it out. I mean, what is it about women wanting to talk a matter to death? I nearly said something stupid, idiotic in fact, and you made it perfectly clear that I'd got the wrong end of the stick. I *get* it."

Although Rose didn't look at him, Flynn saw the pinch of her eyes and watched her heave a deep sigh. She looked like she wanted to reply but didn't. Thank god, they didn't need to analyse his fuck-up.

A few seconds later, Rose led the way beneath the railway bridge. She didn't look at Flynn as she walked. Although they didn't speak, the sound of their footsteps announced their arrival to the town. Not that a small noise mattered, Flynn had no doubt the rats were already watching them.

CHAPTER 14

They were probably being watched. It would have been naive to think otherwise. But they'd walked for about twenty minutes through the town, and as yet, Flynn hadn't seen a single rat. His eyes stung from how hard he searched the shadows. Nothing.

Neither Flynn nor Rose had said a word to one another as they delved deeper into the dark wreck of the place. They'd gone farther in than he'd ever been before.

It looked to Flynn like Rose had followed the *KEEP OUT* signs. Instead of warning them off, they appeared to give them the perfect path to the rats.

When they arrived at an old housing estate, Flynn took the place in, his mouth open wide. It was the residential side of the twisted town.

A wall stood in front of them. It had a gap in it that no doubt had gates across it at some point. The wall was covered in blood-red scrawls; the words *KEEP OUT* repeated over and over. Maybe the rats did know how to write; although it was likely someone else had done it.

The bleached remains of human skeletons littered the

ground. Despite the weak moonlight making it hard to see, when Flynn looked down at the long bones, the teeth marks on them couldn't have been any clearer. Whatever had feasted on them had chewed all the way to the marrow.

Rose stopped a few paces ahead and waited for Flynn to catch up before she said, "Looks like we're here."

"You think?" The housing estate beyond looked like a hellish approximation of suburban living. The underside version of what had once been the British dream. A detached four-bedroom house in a nice gated community. Two cars on a driveway big enough to accommodate them. A small one, no more than a station car that could be left during the day while the worker of the couple commuted to the city, the other one a people carrier for the children and everything that came with them. Sterile living for a sterile existence in corporate Britain.

The windows on every house had been smashed. Doors had been kicked off. Darkness sat deep within every building. An army could be hiding in any one, or even all of them. An army waiting for the right moment to attack.

When Rose stepped forward, Flynn followed her. Where he'd been cold before, he shivered uncontrollably now as fear-induced adrenaline added to the chill in his bones.

They made it to the first house and Flynn copied Rose in pressing his back against the rough wall of it. The coarse brickwork rubbed against his still-healing brand. A duller sting than the one in his wrists, but still there. His bandaged wounds then throbbed when he put his attention on his rope burns. He needed to get them cleaned up soon before the infection got so bad he'd have to amputate his fucking hands.

They moved along the side of the house, deeper into the dark and still estate. The wind and the slight scrapes of their movements were the only sounds in the place. It felt like even the buildings held their breath, waiting for the moment to release chaos on them.

As he walked, Flynn looked up at the first-floor windows. Were he in the rats' position of trying to defend the place, he would have stationed guards high up in the houses. They'd be able to survey the area from up there. But he couldn't see any movement.

Then Rose grabbed Flynn's arm, making him jump. His heart on overdrive, he looked to where she pointed and saw the faint glow of candlelight in one of the downstairs windows of one of the houses.

When Rose looked at Flynn, he pulled a deep breath to calm himself and nodded for her to lead the way.

They crossed an old road to another house before disappearing back into the shadow cast by the tall building. Although they'd exposed themselves a few times already, until they knew they'd been seen, they had to assume they hadn't. And what would the rats do anyway? They'd come here to help liberate them. Surely they'd see that and let them through.

They passed another downstairs window and Flynn winced as he peered into the darkness inside. Although he expected a jack-in-the box shock, he saw no sign of life in there. Maybe all the rats stayed together in the candlelit house. Maybe whoever controlled them had them in some kind of prison they couldn't escape from. Rose had been right to come back here. They couldn't let the suffering continue.

Just a road between them and the candlelit house now, Flynn's throat dried and he fought the urge to appeal to Rose to turn back. Instead, he watched her poke her head out, his stomach tight. She then ran for it, stooping as she crossed over to the candlelit house as if a stoop would hide her in plain sight. If the rats were vigilant, they'd already seen them.

But what else could Flynn do? He peered around the house next and followed her across, running in a crouch like she had.

As she'd done with the other houses, Rose pressed her back to the wall of the lit-up house and Flynn followed. When she got to the brightest window, she peered into the room for the briefest second before quickly pulling back.

Flynn gasped to watch it. Had they seen her?

Rose moved back to Flynn, her eyes wide as she spoke in a whisper. "There's an adult in there, just like we thought."

Before Flynn could respond, Rose moved off again, dropping down onto all fours so she could crawl beneath the window and get to the other side of it, giving him a chance to look in.

The room must have been the house's lounge. Packed with small bodies, they sat around on tatty furniture that had clearly been scavenged from other houses. There looked to be at least fifty grubby kids in there, lit candles dotting the space surrounding them. In the centre of them—like Rose had feared—sat a man on a throne-like chair. A vicious-looking fucker, he slept surrounded by kids. They'd done the right thing in coming back to the town. This couldn't carry on.

After Flynn pulled away from the window, he dropped down onto all fours too.

"This is why we came here," Rose said across the gap beneath the window. She picked up a broken brick from the ground. "If we do nothing else in this town, we have to take that man down. We have to put a stop to this."

They'd come this far, so it made sense. Hopefully the little fuckers would appreciate the gesture and not lynch them afterwards. A deep breath, Flynn said, "Okay. I'll follow your lead."

CHAPTER 15

Flynn set off after Rose towards the front of the house. They were going to burst in through the front door, go straight for the man, and take him down before he had time to react.

Just before he rounded the bend, he moved back to peer in through the window into the living room. And thank god he did. "Shit!" he muttered, dread sending cold prickles up the back of his neck. Just before he could call to Rose, she vanished around the corner towards the front door. "Shit!"

Hard to run and remain quiet, Flynn did his best as he chased after her. If she busted into that house now, they'd be well and truly fucked. They'd gotten it wrong. Their fight wouldn't be them against the man, it would be them against the room full of rats.

Flynn darted around the corner in time to grab Rose's arm just before she reached down for the door handle. She snapped an angry glare at him as he dragged her back, resisting his pull, but not enough that he couldn't get her away. For a moment, she looked like she'd swing for him, but his face must have shown her she needed to listen.

"*What?*" she said when he'd pulled her back around the side of the house.

Out of breath from panic more than anything, Flynn said, "The man isn't holding them hostage."

"What are you talking about?"

"The man's strapped to the chair. His neck, his wrists … The rats have *him* held prisoner, not the other way round."

Before Rose could say anything else, Flynn dragged her back to where they'd been standing before. Close to the window, he pointed at it. "See for yourself. Go on."

While Rose peered into the house, Flynn crawled beneath the window to remain hidden from view. He stood up on the other side and looked in too.

At that moment, the man, who'd had his eyes closed until then, slowly opened them, squinting as if the candlelight in the room dazzled him. Maybe they'd drugged him with something. Although from the size of the welt on his head, it looked like they'd probably just knocked him out.

It took just a few seconds before he opened his eyes wide, the realisation of his situation clearly kicking in. He looked at the children around him, his mouth forming a perfect O of terror. "You little bastards!" he said. "What are you going to do to me?"

The children in the room came to life. A writhe of revulsion curled through Flynn to watch their slow and deliberate movements. Where they'd been dozing, they roused themselves, standing up and shifting across the furniture so they surrounded him. More animal than human, they looked confident in their control of the situation.

The man twisted and jolted in his chair, the wooden feet cracking against the hard floor. Red-faced, he jumped around as much as his restraints would allow and took in the room like he'd not seen it before.

The rats continued to close around him. Silent in their movement, ravenous with their intent.

"What have I done to you?" the man shouted. Not that it made any difference, the rats continued to press in around him with their slow and deliberate crawls.

A glance at Rose showed Flynn the frown on her face. He watched her chew the inside of her mouth before he turned back to the little creatures.

The rats were like a rising tide. Slow, steady, and utterly unstoppable, they converged on the man as his breaths quickened with his panic.

Maybe Flynn should have tried to do something, but what? They were outnumbered by the little fuckers. They wouldn't last two minutes if they challenged them.

When the rats had surrounded the man, they parted slightly for one of the larger children. Old enough to have stubble on his face, he stood at just over six feet tall. Still carrying the skinny frame of a boy, he must have been about fifteen.

As one, the rats dipped their heads in their leader's presence.

The rats had a reputation for liking their prey conscious when they ate them. Although Flynn knew what to expect and twisted most of his body away from the window, he couldn't take his eyes from it.

It looked like the leader was about to kiss the man. He leaned in and turned his head to the side. However, instead of going for his lips, the stubbled teenager opened his mouth wide and bit the man's nose with a crunch.

The sound ran straight to Flynn's stomach and he fought against a heave.

The man released a nasal scream that ran through the estate. The echo died in the night. No one cared. He continued to shake and writhe in his seat, fighting to get free of his bonds. The legs of the chair banged against the hard floor again when he jumped up and down.

A free-for-all, the rats closed in. They'd bowed down to their leader; now they could have their feed. The little beasts converged on the man with their mouths open wide, latching on to whatever part of him they could get to.

Hysterical screams, the man still tried to fight as the rats bit into him. Some of them chomped down on the top of his head as if they could get through his skull.

All the while, Flynn could still see some of the man's face. He watched blood running from his head, the glistening red standing in sharp contrast to the whites of his wide eyes.

The screaming lasted for a few more seconds before the lead rat forced the man's head back and bit into his throat.

A loud gargle, several sharp convulsions, and the man fell limp. A second later, Flynn lost sight of him to the swarm of rats.

By the time Flynn looked back at Rose, slack with the shock from what he'd just seen, he found her staring at him. At least, he thought that was what he saw. After he'd looked at her for a few seconds, he saw she actually looked past him.

A chill in his bones, Flynn fought against his reluctance and turned to see what Rose had. The cold of the night smothered him when he saw it.

The wide and ravenous eyes of a rat stared at them from the front of a nearby house. It had moved out onto the lawn and stood statuesque in its unwavering observation of them. It hunched down like an animal readying an attack.

When it drew a deep breath and opened its mouth wide, time seemed to slow down. Knowing what was coming, but unable to do anything about it, Flynn winced in anticipation of the noise.

The small creature released a cawing sound that made Flynn think of a demented bird. Its shrill call came in waves and rang through the housing estate like the man's scream had. It alerted any and all rats in the area. Not a cry for help, a call to action. It had found two more.

A glance back into the house and Flynn saw the rats had pulled away from the blood-soaked corpse. As one, the hungry and hollow eyes stared straight at him. He and Rose looked at one another before Rose shouted, "Run!"

CHAPTER 16

Flynn ran straight for the noisy rat on the neighbouring front lawn. It stopped to draw breath, giving him a moment to see the reality of what he raced towards. A child, it was no more than eight or nine years old. Not to blame for its actions because it had been socially conditioned to behave in that way. That didn't stop it being a threat to his and Rose's lives.

Then it yelled again. Flynn didn't break stride despite his reservations. He kicked the little fucker square in the face with a loud *crack*. Child or not, it wanted to eat him alive.

The rat flew backwards from the blow, instantly out cold. Flynn jumped over its limp form and took to the roads running through the old housing estate. No need for stealth anymore, he ran with the sound of Rose's footsteps a few metres back.

It took just a few seconds before a rush gave chase behind them. Hundreds of simultaneous footsteps, it sounded like a landslide. A plague. A glance over his shoulder and he saw the mob of wretched little things spill from the candlelit house and several houses behind it. They came through the front doors and through the downstairs windows. Some of them even jumped from the top floors, landing and giving chase as if they were superhuman.

Adrenaline overpowered Flynn's exhaustion as he sprinted through what used to be the front gates of the community. He listened to be sure Rose kept pace with him. Other than that, they needed to focus on their own escape. Despite being together, they were alone on this one.

Although Flynn remembered the way back, the *KEEP OUT* signs helped. They reminded him of his path. A small reassurance as his doubt threatened to climb his tired body and choke him.

The old streets were abandoned. Fortunately, in the town, the roads hadn't given over to the push of grass through them as much as they had elsewhere. Solid underfoot, Flynn moved like the wind down them.

A quick check behind, Flynn saw Rose and, behind her, rats filling the entire width of the road. A tsunami of little feral bodies. Where they'd only seen about fifty in the house, it looked like at least one to two hundred of the little fuckers followed them now.

Flynn fought for breath, his pulse pounding. He heard Rose gain on him, even over the sound of the charge.

The houses on either side had looked abandoned. Until Flynn saw something inside one of them, and then inside several others. Movement. Sunken and hungry eyes peered from the darkness, watching them pass. They then spilled out of the buildings and gave chase with the others.

∽

FIVE TO TEN MINUTES OF RUNNING AND THE SLAP OF FLYNN'S feet echoed through the streets. It might not have revealed anything to the rats, but he knew himself, and even if he ignored the nagging feeling urging him to give up, he couldn't deny the clumsy stamp of his tired steps. If even one of the little fuckers caught up to him, he'd fold like wet card.

The reality of it sent a spike of panic through him. His legs wobbled, but he kept going. His and Rose's lives depended on him getting them out of there. He needed to keep moving.

A few seconds later, Rose caught up to Flynn and they burst out into the high street together. He listened to her rhythmic breath as she moved up to his shoulder: In … two, three, four. Out … two, three, four. He did his best to mimic it; anything to stop his lungs feeling like they were about to burst.

The rats still packed the road and some of them moved through the shops on either side of them. They transitioned from one building to the next at the same pace as him and Rose. They jumped through ground-floor windows, vaulted obstructions, and navigated fallen roofs as some of them ran along the tops of the buildings. If they wanted to, they could clearly outpace the pair. So why hadn't they yet?

The large decrepit tower block stood in plain sight. The symbol of their exit from the town. Chased by the pack of rats who moved like monkeys hunting them through the canopy and funneling them where they wanted them to go, Flynn focused on the old commercial building.

When Flynn and Rose rounded the corner, they saw the railway bridge and stopped dead.

Flynn's legs burned as both he and Rose gasped for breath.

Their path out of the town had been blocked. It seemed like as many rats were packed into the tight space as had chased them. They couldn't get through.

"What do we do?" Rose said, her entire body rocking with her respiration as she tried to recover. She looked over her shoulder at the pack approaching them.

No time to answer, Flynn took off again, running around the other side of the old office block. He'd never been around that side before. And with good reason ...

When Flynn saw the dead end, he slowed his pace. The last of his strength abandoned him. What had once been a wide road leading somewhere now ended abruptly with a mountain of rubble. It looked like a large building on the right had collapsed across the highway, making it impassable. Yet he still continued towards it at a jog. Where else could they go?

It didn't matter how close he got to it, he still couldn't see a way over. A shake of his head and he muttered, "Fuck!"

The rats had slowed down behind them. They blocked the street. They knew they'd won. Hissing and clicking as they stepped forward, many of them bared their teeth at the pair, biting at the air between them as if they could taste them.

The dryness in Flynn's throat made it pinch every time he swallowed. It reached down and grabbed a hold of his gag reflex. He spread his mouth wide to pull as much air in as he could. His wrists buzzed with the sweat that now soaked his bandages.

Rose moved next to him, and together they faced the rats as they backed towards the wall of rubble.

Flynn looked at the crowd of small people and shrugged, keeping his attention on them as he spoke to Rose. "There's nothing for it. We're screwed."

After several heavy breaths, Rose looked across at Flynn and said, "I didn't mean to reject you earlier."

"You want to do this now? Seriously?"

"Learn when to shut up, Flynn."

Even now, with their lives in the balance, Rose's harsh words stung.

"I *like* you," Rose said. "I have since the moment I met you. Why do you think I saved you from going back to the dungeon?"

"What is it, then?"

"I'm scared."

Flynn looked at the rats. They seemed to be enjoying their power, slowing down and edging forwards, almost humouring the pair by pretending they were approaching them with caution.

"I didn't want to get close to another person so they could die on me."

Unable to take his eyes from the mob, Flynn said, "And it looks like you were right. Oh well, it wouldn't have been much of a future even if you had reciprocated. Not with this as our fate."

"I just wanted to say it before …"

"Before we die?"

Rose's bottom lip buckled out of shape, her breaths stuttering from her.

Flynn turned around and pulled a bent piece of rebar from the rubble. He raised it, ready to swing at the rats. Rose did the same.

"Thank you," Flynn said. "I think." A wave of the rebar, he added, "The way I see it, it's better to go down fighting than just wait for them to take us. Let's make these little cunts work for their dinner. Maybe we can take a few of them with us."

When Rose nodded, Flynn stepped forward and shouted, "Come on then, you little shits! Let's fucking have it!"

CHAPTER 17

Flynn moved across in front of Rose so he stood between her and the rats. She was not the kind of woman to do that to, but he did it anyway. If they got out of there, he'd more than happily face her scorn.

The little creatures continued to press forward, hissing and snarling as they came. A clear lack of self-control, one of them broke from the pack and rushed them, snapping its teeth, showing its destructive intent.

Flynn clenched his jaw as he brought the piece of rebar in an uppercut into the rat's chin. It connected cleanly, sending a spray of blood into the air and forcing the kid backwards. It hit the concrete ground with a slap and didn't move. Maybe a bit too much, but he had to send a message to the others.

Another one rushed him. Flynn caught it in the temple and it crumpled with a wet *crunch.*

Two came at them and Rose stepped next to Flynn. As much as he wanted to protect her, he needed her beside him. Together, they dropped the two kids like they were diseased.

To kill the children they'd planned on saving drained more of Flynn's already dwindled energy. He said to the rest of them, "Please, don't make me do this. Just leave us alone and we'll get out of here."

Four came at them this time. Flynn stepped forward and met the one at the front with an overarm blow onto its crown. Its legs buckled, its momentum carrying it forward as it hit the road chin first. In his peripheral vision, he saw Rose deal with her two. She managed it with brutal efficiency.

The next rat dodged Flynn's first attack and kicked his shin on its way past. A sharp sting ran through his lower leg from the impact.

Not a good idea to turn his back on the pack, but he had no other choice than to deal with his aggressor. Flynn led with his bar as he spun around, catching the creature on the side of its face. It burst its eye, the rat clapping a hand to where he'd hit. Despite the heavy blow, the little beast remained on its feet, blood seeping through its small fingers.

The rat snarled and hissed at him, but he saw the truth of it. A wounded animal, it had no more fight left. He stepped aside to let it return to the others. Hopefully it would take the message back with it.

Unfortunately not. An entire line of the little beasts stepped forward this time. A deep breath did nothing to settle Flynn's nerves. They were screwed; it was just a matter of time. There were too many of the small creatures to defeat.

But before any of the kids could rush them, a snarling, wailing sound burst from the press of bodies in the street. Flynn had purposefully ignored the gender of the kids until that moment. It had made them easier to kill. But, for some reason, he couldn't ignore this one. A girl, no older than about seven, ran out in front of the line of rats. She shoved the largest one over and screamed at the others. It came out as a loud, broken wail like that of a madwoman.

The entire line backed off and the girl spun to face Flynn

and Rose.

"She clearly wants us for her own," Flynn said. He raised his rebar and shouted louder than she had. "Come on then, you little shit! You fucking want some?"

Wide-eyed silence met Flynn's challenge.

"I don't think she wants to fight you."

Flynn turned to Rose. "Huh?"

"Look at her. She doesn't look like she wants to fight."

The same dirty skin as every rat. The same sunken and hungry eyes. The same greasy and matted hair. She looked no different than the rest of them, until he recognised her. "You're the girl in the shop," Flynn said. "The one with the cockroach."

A hard scowl crushed the girl's dirty face and she continued to glare at him.

Flynn had seen that same scowl when she'd grabbed the cockroach. "You were part of the mob that waited for me to leave so you could attack Serj."

A strong breeze ripped down the street, throwing the smell of dirt at Flynn. The smell of hundreds of filthy bodies. He ruffled his nose at the stench. "What do you want?" he said.

His words seemed to break through the girl's facade and she dropped her fierce stare for a second. When she looked up again, she moved her mouth as if chewing something she couldn't clear from the back of her throat. A guttural growl came from her like she was trying to form sounds she'd never heard before.

A shimmer ran through the rats behind her, almost as if they were gearing up to attack again. They could spring to life at any moment, regardless of what the girl wanted. Flynn's and Rose's lives rested firmly in their hands; the rebar clubs would only get them so far.

Flynn squeezed a tighter grip on the heavy metal pole, the corkscrew twist of it easier to hold in his sweaty hand. They were getting nowhere fast.

When the girl tried to speak again, Flynn felt like he understood her. At first, it had sounded like nothing, but when he focused, he could hear something of a shared language hiding within the noise. He asked, "The man in the house?"

The girl nodded.

"The one we saw tied up? The man you all just killed, you mean?"

Heavy breaths rocked the girl's slight frame. She'd fight if he wanted it. Despite her size, she'd rip his fucking throat out if he pushed her too far. A dip of her head and she looked up at him from beneath her brow, the whites of her sunken eyes stark against her dirty skin. The sounds of her words echoed in the space, the other rats silent as she spoke. "Bad man!"

"The man in the house was a bad man?"

A deep breath lifted her frame and the girl almost spat the words, but they became clearer every time she spoke. "He tried to hurt us."

Flynn looked at the rats behind her. They'd all stepped forward. He fought to keep the panic from his words. "Okay, let's say I believe that. That you only kill people who deserve it. Is that what you're trying to say?"

Just one short sharp nod to agree with his statement.

Anger rose in Flynn and he fought not to shout at her. "Then what about Serj? He didn't try to hurt you."

A genuine twist of confusion ran through the girl's face. Shame, embarrassment, hurt. "Offering," she said.

"You what?" Flynn laughed ironically. "You thought Serj was an offering to you?"

Another shrug. "Dead anyway."

To talk about Serj sped Flynn's breaths up again, so he took a moment as he watched the pack of rats close in another step. They were no more than two metres from them at that point. Just one spark and they'd burst to life.

Maybe the girl had a point. They'd taken plenty of offerings to the town before. They might not have taken bodies to them, but other communities could have.

The girl pressed the palms of her hands together in prayer and dipped a bow at Flynn. She looked unsure of herself for the first time, like she didn't understand the meaning of their conversation. "We thank you for offering."

Not an offering, but he needed to let it slide. The fall had killed Serj. *He'd* killed Serj. The kids just benefitted from the accident.

"We leave you now," the girl said.

A quick glance at Rose, Flynn saw she still held her rebar ready to use it. He then turned back to watch the girl spin around and face the crowd. Her scream—louder than when she'd burst into the fight—damn near shook the foundations of the surrounding buildings.

Flynn jumped from the sound and looked at Rose again. She had the palm of her left hand pressed against her chest as if to calm her heart. She hadn't yet lowered her bar.

The pack of rats kept their eyes on Flynn and Rose, but they backed away from them. Slowly, cautiously, they pulled out of the road they'd filled, showing they would give them a route out of there.

While standing and watching the kids clear out, Flynn flinched when Rose reached down and held his free hand. When she squeezed, the smallest amount of tension left his body. He squeezed back. Maybe they would get out of there after all.

CHAPTER 18

The town and the rats behind them, Flynn kept a hold of Rose's hand as they walked towards the barn they'd been in a few hours previously. The large structure stood as it had before, a dark silhouette to focus on in the blanket of night. Just the slightest silver highlight from the moon ran along its apex like a line of chalk.

A couple of times it felt to Flynn like Rose might let go of his hand. Not wanting to appear desperate, he'd let her, but he kept a grip to try to encourage her to hold on. Especially now she'd told him she liked him too.

What she had said to him in the town made sense; the world had screwed her up and made her standoffish. Not on the surface, but it made it hard for her to get close to anyone. He understood it. The new world had fucked over most people. He just needed to give her some time to come out of her shell. If he stayed there for her, everything would work out.

"We tried to save the rats," Flynn said, breaking the silence between them.

Although Rose turned to look at him, the swish of the grass yielding to their fast march, she didn't say anything.

"Do you ever wonder if ..." Flynn paused for a moment and stared into Rose's eyes. "I dunno ... If maybe we've got it wrong?"

"What do you mean?"

"Well, look how that just turned out. We nearly died trying to do the right thing. Were it not for that little girl, we'd have been fucked." And he'd have lost Rose.

Again Rose didn't reply. The barn held her attention as they walked towards it, the ground uneven underfoot.

Flynn needed to give her space and time. To tell her he was petrified of losing her would be too much too soon.

The cold, night-time dew trebled the weight of Flynn's trousers and soaked the bandages covering his wrists. The chilled press gave some relief to his throbbing wounds, but it probably did nothing to keep them free from infection. God knew what they looked like under the bandages at that moment.

"Maybe we should focus on getting as far away from here and the Queen as possible," Flynn said.

Another few seconds passed without a response from Rose. Although Flynn inhaled to speak again, she said, "I don't want to live in that world, Flynn."

"You'd rather die in this one?"

A look at Rose and Flynn saw the tears in her eyes. "I'm sorry. I didn't mean to snap at you. I'm scared." He had to say it now. "I like you. And now I know you like me too, I don't want to lose that."

After another moment's pause, Rose said, "When Mum helped me get free from the people attacking us, she told me to always stand in the light and do the right thing. The only guide I have now is my moral compass. If I listen to that, everything will work out for the best. We had the right intention with the rats and it worked out."

"Worked out?"

"We're alive."

"Not by design. We were lucky."

Rose shrugged, lifting Flynn's hand with her action. "Luck … fate … what's the difference?"

"Luck just happens. Fate is a lie we tell ourselves."

Rose remained calm and shook her head. "But I don't believe it is. And you know what? What does it matter even if it is a lie? If it's a placebo? Better to trust everything will be okay—"

"Than plan for it? Sounds a bit wishy-washy to me."

"You're not getting it." Rose let go of Flynn's hand and pulled her long blonde hair away from her face. "I always *intend* to do the right thing. *Always*. But that's all I have. It's naive to think I can predict how things will work out. That I can plan for the complex algorithm that's life. Control's an illusion, Flynn. The more you try to hold onto it, the more distressed you become."

Flynn frowned hard as they walked, but he didn't respond. "So you're telling me I'm powerless in this world?"

"Intention is a powerful thing. I'm telling you that nothing ever goes *exactly* as planned. Ever. Even if it's just the minor details. If I always intend to do the right thing, I have to trust that everything else will be okay beyond that. And you know what? One day it probably won't be. But there's no point in pretending I can predict that, or prepare for it, just like there's no point in pretending I can predict anything."

It hurt Flynn's head to find fault with her argument.

"I'm not saying don't do anything. Because without action, there can't be a reaction. And sometimes those reactions are an approximation of what we hoped for. But there's also no point in lying to ourselves about having control over this world." She paused for a second. "It took facing the end of my life in the town to tell you how I feel about you. I should have told you that sooner. I should have had faith. I'm sorry I waited until then. Sometimes it's not so easy to follow your own advice, eh? Anyway, my point is the sooner you let go of focusing on the results and focus on your intention, the sooner you'll find peace."

"Peace? In this world? With all the shit that's happened?"

"Peace and pain aren't mutually exclusive. Things have happened as they've happened. I can't change the fact that my mum's dead." Rose took a moment to compose herself. A solitary tear ran down her cheek, carrying the silver glow of the moon with it. "But I can accept it. I can know that I did what I could at the time, and if I was back in that moment, I would make exactly the same choice because that was the choice I made then. Acceptance is all I have now."

As much as he didn't want to admit it, it made sense. If he'd had a chance to relive Vicky and Serj dying, he wouldn't have been able to change it. The information of how to prevent both of them only came to him after they'd passed.

"Also," Rose said, "even if I didn't have these beliefs, my mum told me to be the change I wanted to see in the world. To stand in the light. I believe that's a good way to live my life, and she asked it of me as her dying wish. She died to save me. The least I can do is honour her request."

Flynn drew a breath to respond, but Rose cut him off. "This isn't a philosophy that's come easy for me. Mum didn't just die. They didn't simply cut her throat like they did with the others. Several of the men ..." A shake ran through Rose and she cried more freely than before.

"It's okay," Flynn said and grabbed her hand again. It felt

cold to the touch. "You don't have to say it. It's okay." He then moved closer to Rose and put his arm around her.

"I need to do the right thing, Flynn. I can't stress out about a fictional prediction of what could go wrong. If I'm to live through this, I need to do what I know is right. You need to decide what your path is. I'll understand if you want to go your own way, but the Queen has people that we know are being tortured and oppressed, and she plans to attack the people of Home; as far as I'm concerned, I have to do what I can to stop her."

CHAPTER 19

~~~

Cold and tired, Flynn held Rose's hand as they stumbled into the barn.

Like in the town, the rough concrete ground had held up against the grass' unrelenting determination, and it had no cracks in it. Both Flynn's and Rose's steps scuffed over the ground as they walked to the same corner Flynn had sat down in earlier that evening.

They sat close to one another, their backs pressed against the hard wooden wall along one side of the structure. The darkness hung so complete that when Flynn looked into a corner on the opposite side of the space, it seemed to leech the light from his eyes. Although, when he looked at the doorway, he could see the top of the long grass as it swayed in the wind. The moonlight might have been weak, but compared to where they found themselves at that moment, it shone like a lamp.

Flynn sat shoulder to shoulder with Rose and couldn't tell where his shivering ended and hers began. They'd both been soaked by the dewy grass during their walk back from the town.

Other than the sound of the wind outside, Flynn couldn't hear anything—until Rose spoke.

"Thank you for coming back to the town with me. You didn't have to."

The first time they'd stopped for what felt like days, Flynn's eyelids grew heavy as he shrugged. "I know, but I wanted to be with you. Even if that meant going in there."

The slur in Rose's words revealed her fatigue, and her actions were clumsy as she reached over and found his hand. "Thank you."

It looked like there was movement out in the meadow, causing Flynn to sit up straighter, but Rose didn't seem to notice. But as he stared out of the barn, he couldn't see anything. It had to be his imagination; it would have been rare to see hunters or nomads, almost unheard of to meet them both on the same day. No way would there be anyone else outside.

Rose gave Flynn's hand a gentle squeeze. "Do you think I'm nuts for saying all that stuff about intention and control? I've suffered with a lot of anxious thoughts. It's the only way I've found to help stay calm."

"It makes sense. And although I may have been resistant at first, I'm on board. What's the point of this life if we can't try to make it better? I learned that from Vicky. She died trying to make my life better. So did my mum and dad. We should be doing the same for the generations coming after us."

A short pause and Rose spoke with a small voice as if nervous to ask the question. "What happened with your mum and dad?"

Before Flynn knew it, he'd heaved a weary sigh. He kept his focus outside.

"You don't have to tell me," Rose said. "I was just curious."

A shake of his head and Flynn said, "No, it's fine. Did I tell you how Dad saved us all?"

"No."

The slightest smile lifted one side of Flynn's mouth. "If ever there was a story of a hero …"

Rose turned and looked up at Flynn. He drew a deep breath to gather his thoughts. "He was right by the Alpha Tower when the virus broke out. He and Mum were separated at that point. When he saw the chaos, he had just one thing on his mind: he had to get me. I was only six at the time. Although heroic in his efforts, he was also lucky to bump into Vicky, who was running out of the city. Because she knew about the virus, she knew exactly what was coming and which way they needed to run. The pair of them fought their way out towards my school on the outskirts."

"It must have been insane," Rose said.

"They told me it was. I don't remember because I was too young." The hypnotic sway of the long grass outside the barn made Flynn zone out. After blinking his drowsiness away, he continued. "Apparently, when they got to my school, everyone had been taken down by the virus. They thought I'd died and nearly gave up on me. Then Dad remembered how I loved to climb a specific tree. He checked it and they found me up it. I was the only survivor from hundreds."

"And what about your mum? How did you save her?"

A strong breeze swung into the place and Flynn tensed against its chill. "She worked in Summit City too. Apparently, all the tower blocks had anti-terrorist shields around them. As soon as the virus broke out, the city went into lockdown. That may have been okay in itself, but because the disease broke out on an island, they'd set up Summit City to incinerate to try to contain the virus. Dad might have been inclined to leave Mum in there, but apparently I said I wanted her with me. He risked his life to make sure that happened and went back into the diseased city."

"He went back in? That would have been suicidal!"

"I'm not sure he gave it much thought. He always said to me that if I ever have a child, I'd understand. How from the second I was born, he lived to serve me. And how he wouldn't have been able to live with himself for not getting Mum back to me."

"What if he'd failed?"

"He said he didn't think about it."

"He focused on his intention because he couldn't control the outcome."

Flynn smiled. "Right. After that we survived. We survived for the longest time. At least ten years. We lived in shipping containers." He ruffled his nose at the memory of it. "The one we all used for a toilet stank. Although, the diseased constantly around us didn't help with the stench either."

At that moment, Rose moved closer to Flynn and snuggled into his chest. He put his arm around her. In the process, he knocked his left wrist. An electric streak of pain ran up him and he pulled a sharp breath in through his clenched teeth.

"We need to clean your wounds up and re-dress them," Rose said.

Flynn nodded. They did. "In the morning."

"So what happened?"

"Vicky said she wanted to leave. To move on. Mum and Dad were back together for years and I think she felt like a spare wheel. I was sixteen then. She said I was old enough to go out scavenging with Dad, and they didn't need her anymore."

The hard and cold ground turned Flynn's arse numb, but he didn't want to move in case Rose moved too. Better to have her there and be uncomfortable. A slight shift and he continued, "Vicky promised to come out on a scavenging mission with us one last time before she left. That was when it happened."

Despite it happening a long time ago, the pain of it rose in Flynn as a rock in his throat. He gulped against it, but couldn't chug it down. After feeling another warm squeeze of his hand from Rose, he continued. "When we were out scavenging, we went near a stream." He paused for a moment to gather himself. "I'd been living in shipping containers for years. They hadn't had time to teach me to swim."

"You fell in?" Rose asked.

"And Dad rescued me. He got me out of the stream, but the diseased must have heard my struggle because they suddenly appeared and jumped on him. He told me to run and Vicky dragged me away. They'd already bitten him by that point."

"I'm so sorry," Rose said. "How awful."

The images in Flynn's mind were as fresh as if he'd seen them yesterday. "When Mum found out, I think she still thought Vicky planned to move on. She went out on her own to try to scavenge. She didn't tell either of us she planned to do it. I think she thought she'd need to support both of us when Vicky left. But because Dad had died, Vicky had changed her mind about going."

"She just hadn't told her?"

"No." The tears came at that moment and Flynn shook harder than before. Still looking outside at the long grass with the silver highlight, he said, "We woke up to find her banging on the shipping containers with the rest of the diseased." His bottom lip buckled out of shape. "She looked as desperate to get to us as the others were. It was the first time I saw the evil twist of familiarity in a diseased. I saw the face of a loved one hell-bent on my destruction."

"My god."

A warm trickle of tears ran down Flynn's face and he shook with gentle sobs. After drawing a stuttered breath, he laughed and shook his head. "I'm sorry. I didn't think it would upset me like this."

Another warm squeeze of his hand, Rose said, "It's okay. You don't need to talk about it anymore. So, tomorrow …"

"Yep."

"We're going to go to the royal complex?"

A wet sniff against his running nose and Flynn nodded in the darkness. "Yeah, it seems like the best bet."

When Rose turned to look up at Flynn, he quickly wiped his tears away. "Thank you," she said.

"For what?" Flynn frowned as he stared down at her, straight into her dark eyes. Despite the lack of light in the barn, the slightest glow from the moon showed him her beautiful gaze.

"For telling me about your family. For opening up. For trusting in me and understanding who I am. I've not had that before from someone." Rose reached up and wiped his tears away with her thumb.

As they stared at one another, the urge to lean down and kiss Rose tugged on Flynn's neck. But he didn't. What if she didn't feel ready for that? He needed her in his arms after dragging up the memories of his family. He smiled at her and then looked back out of the barn. "I think it's best we both get some sleep. We have a lot to do in the morning."

CHAPTER 20

The sun shone through the large space where the doors to the barn had once been. A strong beam of light and heat pressed against Flynn's face, forcing him awake. When he opened his eyes, they burned from the glare, so he snapped them shut again. A slight headache throbbed through his temples from where he'd been cooking for however long it had taken him to wake.

Flynn pulled in a deep breath as if it would help him transition from his dreamy state. The smell of rotting wood surrounded him. How long would it be before the barn collapsed?

Another attempt, Flynn opened his eyes more slowly than before, letting in the bright glare of the early morning.

Because of the daylight, Flynn saw the inside of the barn better than he had the previous evening. Pinpricks of light shone through the old walls where rot had taken chunks from it.

As Flynn woke up, he felt the numbness in his arse and the angry twist to his back. Although, when he looked down to see Rose still hugging him, he smiled. It had been worth the pain.

The same ache he'd had for the past day throbbed through Flynn's wrists. No doubt they'd be excruciating when he moved them.

The cold night had done little to dry out Flynn's joggers and T-shirt, but at least the sun shone. It wouldn't take long outside to banish the damp press of his clothes. Another look out through the barn's doors and he stared at the long grass lit up and swaying in the gentle breeze.

From where he sat, Flynn could see the top of Rose's head and her button nose. He leaned down to kiss her crown. Maybe he should have gone for it last night. She'd as good as given him the green light in the town when the rats closed in on them. But she also thought they were going to die at that moment and had cooled off a little when they managed to get free. They had time; he didn't need to be pushy.

Then Rose stirred, inhaling the first deep breath of waking. Flynn pulled his lips back from the top of her head, heat flushing his cheeks. "Morning," he said, his voice croaky from sleep. He shouldn't try to kiss her. Things were good as they were. He didn't need the pain of another rejection.

It took Rose a few seconds to wake up enough to turn around and look at him. A wonky smile, she then pulled away from him and sat upright.

Before Flynn could say anything, Rose frowned and looked down at his wrists. One of the last thoughts she'd voiced before falling asleep last night resurfaced as she said, "We need to get them re-dressed. The bandages are filthy."

And they were. Rose had done a good job dressing them when they were in the cage in the royal complex, but since then, they'd picked up all kinds of stains. Blood, dirt, grass …

When Rose got to her feet, Flynn couldn't help but stare at her bottom in her joggers. Such a fine woman, sometimes he didn't know where to look without blushing.

Rose reached her hand down to Flynn when she turned to face him, a slight twist of a smile on her lips. She knew he watched her in that way. And why should he be ashamed of being physically attracted to her? She'd made it clear she liked him too. Flynn took her hand and she pulled him to his feet.

When they were both standing, Rose kept a hold of Flynn's hand, moving up to his wrist and the bandage around it. She undid the one on his left wrist first, slowly unwinding it as if she felt every jolt of his pain.

Just the thought of Rose touching his wounds forced Flynn to wince. He watched her unravel the damp and dirty fabric before flinching away from what he anticipated to be a horrible sight. Although, when he looked back, he said, "It's not as bad as I thought."

"It looks pretty grim to me," Rose said.

Flynn said, "Sure, it's dirty and bloody, but I was expecting worse. I thought I'd be able to see the bone. It certainly felt like it when I was working the bonds free." No more than a red cuff, it looked like it would heal just fine with some love and attention.

"We need to clean these cuts out," Rose said.

The dark ring around Flynn's left wrist definitely needed cleaning. No doubt the other one looked the same. "With what?"

Rose didn't look up as she unwound the bandage on his other wrist.

It looked similar to the first one. "Now I've seen them both," Flynn said, "they hurt less. When I thought I'd done some serious damage, my paranoia dragged my thoughts to them all the time. The mind has a funny way of playing tricks, doesn't it?"

But Rose didn't respond. Instead, she lifted the bottom of her T-shirt to her mouth, exposing everything beneath like she'd done in the cage at the royal complex.

Despite knowing he shouldn't, Flynn stared at her pert breasts and said, "Um …"

But Rose ignored him as she bit a strip from her top. The tear of the fabric ripped through the large barn. Flynn looked out through the open space where the doors should have been. He couldn't see anyone outside, but that could change.

"We don't have any water," Rose said, her teeth clamped onto her T-shirt so she could pull another strip free, "but at least we can put fresh bandages on them."

Rose focused on Flynn's left wrist first as she lifted it up. When she leaned close to it, he could see down her top. As much as he wanted to stare, he looked up at the barn's ceiling instead. She'd respect him more for looking away.

Because Flynn had only ever been with Angelica, a dryness spread through his mouth and throat. An attempt to swallow it down felt like swallowing cotton wool.

When Rose finished, she looked up at Flynn and he looked back at her. She'd dropped her T-shirt back down so it covered her. The torn garment looked more like a crop top now.

"I could have given you some of my T-shirt," Flynn said.

"What, you don't think the shorter top suits me?"

The dryness returned to his mouth and he said nothing.

Rose laughed and silence hung between them for a few seconds. She finally said, "I guess we need to head to the royal complex, then?"

The reality of what they had to face sobered Flynn up. He nodded and spoke with a sigh. "Yeah. I guess we should."

CHAPTER 21

The sun still had a long way to climb in the sky before it reached its zenith. During his stay in Home where there had been a working clock, Flynn had gotten used to what different times of day looked like during different seasons. If he had to guess, he'd say it was about nine in the morning.

It was hard to tell exactly, but it had taken them maybe three hours to walk there. They'd moved through the meadows without incident. No hunters, nomads, or rats along the way. And no sign of the Queen and her crew.

They now stood on the brow of a hill, looking down at the royal complex. "I reckon they're still having breakfast," Flynn said. As confident as he tried to sound, his courage had started to slip away from him. To see the vast community in front of them reminded him just how hard it would be to get in there. There seemed little point in hiding it from Rose. "I'd forgotten how well fortified this place is. We've got our work cut out."

Rose stood next to him, squinting against the wind and

the sun as she bore the full force of it. Her long blonde hair blew away from her and the thin fabric of her crop top pressed against her form. A deep frown, she watched on as if contemplating how they'd take the place down. "We definitely need to get the prisoners from the town," she finally said. "No way are we getting back in there on our own. And even with a small army …" She let the sentence fly away on the breeze.

From where they stood, Flynn could see everything: the hospital building—which had definitely seen better days, but still remained standing—the barn in the middle of the complex where the Queen insisted everyone went twice a day, the large tree close to the barn, and the cage they'd strung them up in still hanging down from its branch.

The area surrounding the complex looked like most meadows. A sea of long grass, it bent and swayed, yielding to the elements. "Where do you think we should wait for them to come out?" Flynn said. "I can't see anywhere to hide down there."

But Rose didn't respond.

When Flynn followed her line of sight down to the complex, his stomach sank to see them emerge from the other side of the barn. "They've got their horses back already?"

It took a few seconds for all of them to appear. What seemed to be most of the hunters and royal guards were mobilising. They looked like they were preparing to go out somewhere with a distinct purpose.

"From what I've seen," Rose said, "she treats the horses well. I'm guessing they decided to come back to her. Probably about the only living things that would choose to be in her company."

A loud call sounded out from the guards stationed by the complex's exit and Flynn jumped. A second later the large gates creaked and groaned as they started to open. He dropped down into the long grass and dragged Rose with him.

The meadow served as the perfect shield to hide them from sight. Flynn raised his head enough to be able to see, but remain invisible to those leaving the complex. The first of the horses stepped out into the meadow. It looked like Mistress' guards—Mistress' guards minus Mistress.

"I suppose where we hide is a decision we don't need to think about now," Rose said.

"But what if they come our way?"

"That would be quite unlucky. They could head in any direction, and they'd have to get quite close to see us. Besides, you say it like we have a choice."

Another flutter of anxiety took charge of Flynn's heart.

It seemed to take forever, but the pack of riders outside the complex swelled until it looked like all of the hunters and guards had stepped out to join them. When Flynn saw the Queen, his breath caught in his throat. Surrounded by guards in royal blue, she sat on her horse with a straight back, her nose in the air. He tasted the bitter tang of bile at the sight of her. She'd get hers.

The horses at the front of the pack led them away from the complex in the opposite direction to Flynn and Rose.

"Do you think they're going to the town?" Rose said.

"I think it's in that direction," Flynn replied. "Hard to tell because they blindfolded me. But we would have passed it on the way if it was this side of the complex, right?"

Rose nodded.

The horses might have been far away, but when they quickened their pace, the thunder of their hooves rolled over the landscape like a brewing storm. "Come on," Flynn said when all the horses had galloped away. He stood up and Rose stood up with him.

They walked back down the hill away from the complex. If they were to follow them, they had to find a less obvious path than the one that led them in plain sight of the guards on the gate.

CHAPTER 22

The ridge Flynn and Rose had moved to the other side of ran all the way down past the front of the royal complex. They remained out of sight and walked in the same direction the riders had gone in. Hopefully they'd catch up to them at some point.

About twenty minutes had passed and they hadn't spoken much. They'd moved at a quick pace that made breathing a hard enough task for Flynn. Rose had always seemed fitter than him, but even she glistened with sweat from the rapidly warming day.

At the top of another steep hill, Flynn stopped and wiped his brow. The wind cooled him a little, but not enough to escape the oppressive heat.

Because they hadn't spoken much, when Rose suddenly grabbed Flynn and hissed, "Wait," he jumped, a jolt of panic spiking through him at her urgency.

Flynn watched Rose drop down into the long grass and copied her. Then he saw what she'd seen.

Two people walked through the meadow below them about two hundred metres away. A man and a woman, they looked to be moving down a well-trodden path, the grass flattened all the way along it.

"Is that woman pregnant?" Rose said.

How hadn't he seen it? "Yes." Flynn stared at the woman and her large bump. "Very."

Now he'd stopped, more sweat poured from Flynn's brow. He wiped it away several times in quick succession to stop the saline trickle into his eyes.

"Where do you think they're going?" Rose asked.

"I don't know. It looks like they're following a route plenty of others have walked before them. A lot of people must have trodden that path for the grass to remain flattened." Before Rose could reply to him, Flynn noticed something along the path. "Are those signs?"

A few seconds of silence and Flynn watched Rose squint as she looked where he had. "I think they are. What do you think they say?"

A sinking dread dropped through Flynn. "I think we should follow them and see where they're going. Maybe we can stop them from making a big mistake."

Although she didn't reply to him, Rose moved off through the grass at a low crouch. Flynn followed. It swayed from their movement, but if the two people below looked up, it wouldn't seem like anything other than the wind. Hopefully.

∾

By the time they'd travelled about fifty metres closer to the pathway the couple walked down, Flynn's legs and back ached. Sweat gushed from him, itching around the collar of his thin and filthy T-shirt.

The strong sun pushed down on Flynn's head and his

throat had turned bone dry. The start of a headache bit into his eyes. He needed to find water soon.

Rose moved through the grass a few metres ahead and she stopped first.

When Flynn caught up to her, he could see the signs much better. Lumps of wood attached to stakes, they'd been speared into the ground and all bore a similar message. The painted mess looked like the person barely knew how to write, but they were legible, just.

Come and live in a safe community.
We have food and water.
We look after one another.
The war is over, time for peace.
We have shelter.

Many more signs lined the path and they all offered similar promises. A glance at Rose, Flynn wiped his brow again as he waited for her to finish reading them. When she did, she dropped her head with a sigh before looking back at him. "The Queen."

"Fuck," Flynn said. "I was worried it would be. So this is how she fills her dungeon. We have to stop them before they get to her."

CHAPTER 23

Flynn and Rose moved alongside the path, duckwalking through the long grass. They remained far enough away not to be seen. "I'm going to run to them now," Rose said.

A shake of his head, Flynn reached out and grabbed the top of her arm, "Don't be too hasty. We've got time. Let's see where they're going. We'll stop them before they get into trouble."

Although Rose watched him for a few seconds and looked like she'd say something, she didn't. Instead, she dipped a nod at him. They'd get to the couple before the Queen did. They had time to stop them from making a big mistake.

The couple then disappeared from view as they followed the path over a small hill. Flynn saw Rose about to stand up, so he grabbed her arm again and pulled her back down. "If they turn around, we'll be exposed. We *have* to keep low. We'll catch up to them in a minute, I promise."

Sweat stung Flynn's eyes. It came from his brow in a torrent, so he'd given up wiping it away. The duckwalk ran pains all the way through his thighs up into his lower back. Too much longer and he'd have to stop and rest.

Neither Flynn nor Rose spoke as they quickened their pace. The effort left no room for conversation.

Close to the brow of the hill, Flynn stopped and Rose paused a second later. When she looked at him, he cupped his ear to encourage her to listen.

Rose's eyes spread wide. It told him she'd heard them too. Voices. The couple had run into a group of people on the other side.

What little strength Flynn had left in him went and he slowly folded to the ground. They were too late. They didn't have time like he thought they did.

Rose sat down too, her mouth partly open as she fought to recover her breath.

They both listened to the voices on the other side for a few seconds before Flynn said, "I can't hear what they're saying, can you?"

Rose shook her head.

Curiosity overpowered fatigue and Flynn crawled closer to the sounds with Rose next to him. The second he saw it, he knew Rose must have too.

"Shit!" she said.

It looked like all of the hunters and guards from the royal complex. They remained on their horses, surrounding the two people Flynn and Rose had watched walk through the field. The couple were no more than twenty metres away. But as far as saving them went, they might as well have been on the opposite side of the planet.

The woman cradled her bump, her mouth open wide as she looked up at all the riders. The man spun on the spot, his fists clenched, but lowered at his sides.

"What is this?" the man finally said, his voice carrying through the small valley.

The riders parted and the Queen came forward on her

horse. To see her so close ran tension through Flynn's stomach, and his tired body shook. Thank god he'd never had to fuck her.

"You followed our signs, then?" the Queen said.

"Of course." The man paused and looked at the riders again. "They promised a *friendly* community." It sounded almost like a question.

A sadistic smile spread across the Queen's angular face. "And they spoke the truth." She looked at the riders and laughed. "We're friendly, aren't we?"

Some laughed with her; others simply nodded. None of them spoke, and many of them held onto the handles of their sheathed weapons as if ready to draw them.

"About as friendly as a disturbed wasp's nest," Flynn said beneath his breath.

"Look," the pregnant woman said, her words coming out quickly, "if we've got this wrong, we can turn around and head back."

"You'd like to do that, wouldn't you?" the Queen said.

The woman burst into tears. "Please, I'm pregnant."

For a few seconds, the Queen didn't reply. Instead, she stared down at the pregnant woman, a strange twist to her features as if she was in pain. Then she shook her head, her black hair blowing out behind her. The moment of what might have been compassion vanished. "Oh, I can see that, princess." She sneered as she looked at the man. "Yours, is it?" She looked down at his crotch as if he had a diseased cock.

When Flynn saw the man raise his balled fists, his entire frame sank and he whispered, "Don't rise to it." Part of him wanted to run down there and help them out like Rose had suggested. The couple didn't know what they were up against. They were about to make a huge mistake.

"Look," the man said and Flynn shook his head with a sigh. Especially when the man pointed up at the Queen, his face twisted and red. "I don't know who the fuck you think you are, but if you don't want to let us into your community, that's fine. Just let us through and we'll be on our way."

"Oh, we'll let you into our community, all right," the Queen said. "You just need to prove you're the right kind of person to be let in. We look after our own, so once you've passed a simple test, you can join us. You'll be as good as family after that."

The man looked at the pregnant woman before returning his attention to the Queen. "A *test*? Who made you the boss, you twisted bitch."

Flynn watched tension snap through the riders and they all looked at the Queen as if waiting for the nod.

But the Queen didn't give it. Instead, she smiled. "I'm the Queen. Everyone knows that."

The woman turned to the man and said, "Come on, Dave, let's get out of here."

The riders closed in tighter around them. Were it not for his elevated position, Flynn wouldn't have been able to see the man and woman because of the close press of horses.

"Let us pass," Dave said through a clenched jaw.

"Or what?" the Queen replied.

Dave spun on the spot, taking in the riders surrounding them.

When he didn't speak, the Queen laughed. "I'm not sure you're in a position to be making demands, David."

The pregnant woman cried more freely than before as she looked up at the Queen, her face ugly with her grief. She continued to hold her pregnant belly.

"How long do you have left, dear?" the Queen asked her, her glazed stare fixed on the woman's stomach.

The woman pulled her brown hair behind her ear and continued to cry.

"A couple of weeks at the most," Dave said. He spoke it like an accusation.

The Queen spun on him, shouting so loud, her call disturbed a flock of birds in a nearby tree. "I didn't ask you!"

Even with the distance and the horses between them, Flynn saw Dave clench his jaw. He still had his fists balled, but he didn't reply. A scorned child, he had to swallow his shame and accept her authority.

Other than the sound of the wind, silence swept across the grassy meadow and the Queen continued to focus on the pregnant woman. "Well?"

Her words came out in stuttered bursts. "Two-two-two weeks."

"I'm sorry?" the Queen said and leaned forwards. "Is that *two* weeks, or *two-two-two* weeks?"

The riders around the Queen laughed again, and the woman stared at the ground as she spoke. "Two weeks."

"Well, that's fine, sweetheart. You will have proven your worth to us by then. We have a hospital, you know."

The woman looked up again, the sun glistening off her tear-sodden face. "Please, just let us move on. We wanted to get somewhere safe to have our baby. We're not in any state to go through trials now. Look at me."

"Oh, I am, honey." the Queen said. "And *you* might not be in a fit state, but *he* is. He clearly has quite a lot of fight in him too. I like them feisty."

Dave ran at the Queen.

Before he'd made two steps, one of the royal guards slipped from her horse and drove an uppercut into his chin. It knocked him backwards. The pregnant woman screamed as he crashed to the ground.

A wider smile than before, the Queen tutted several times and shook her head. "Oh dear. It looks like he couldn't control his temper. I kind of figured. He came across as an angry little man. Shame, really, I was excited to see how he'd do in the trials."

Several more royal guards slipped from their horses and surrounded Dave. He got to his feet, shifted backwards, and looked up at the Queen. "Just let us go, you crazy bitch."

"Tie their hands," the Queen said.

One of the royal guards produced two short lengths of rope from her belt. She threw a length at another guard and they both walked over to Dave and the woman.

The pregnant woman continued to sob as they bound her wrists in front of her. They bound Dave's wrists behind his back.

Once they'd done that, the Queen smiled down at Dave as she said to her guards, "You know what to do with him."

Another length of rope appeared and they tied Dave's feet at the ankles. They didn't do the same to the woman.

The guard with the ropes then went to her horse and pulled two longer pieces of rope free from her saddle. Each piece stretched at least five metres long.

The guard tied one end of each rope to the Queen's saddle. She then tied the other ends to the pregnant woman's wrists and Dave's bound ankles.

"What the fuck are you doing?" Dave said as he looked from his feet to the Queen's horse and back again.

"Quite the talker, aren't we?" the Queen said.

Dave pursed his lips and glared at her.

After the guard had tested the knots on both ropes with a sharp tug—Dave having to jump forward when she tested his —the Queen shouted at the riders. "Let's go to the town."

The ropes tied to Dave and the woman pulled taut as the

Queen rode off. The woman stepped forward with them while Dave hopped, his ankles bound too tight for him to shuffle.

Two more hops and Dave lost his balance, his feet dragged from beneath him. He hit the rough ground with an *oomph*, landing on the base of his spine.

Flynn winced to watch him get dragged over the hard ground, his shirt riding up as he shouted again, "You can't do this to me. I won't last two fucking minutes like this."

The Queen stopped and Flynn drew a sharp intake of breath when she turned around. The temperature had dropped as if she controlled the weather. Malice lit up her face. She then grinned her familiar wicked grin. "That's the idea, petal."

CHAPTER 24

They waited in the long grass until the Queen and her army were out of sight. In a matter of minutes, the weather had changed, the temperature continuing to drop as clouds blocked the sun. Flynn looked at Rose and let out a heavy sigh. His tiredness sat in him like he had rocks for bones. "I should have let you go to them."

Rose got to her feet and held her hand down to him to help him up. "You weren't to know. If I hadn't caught them in time, we would have run into the Queen too."

"You would have caught them in time."

After jabbing her hand towards him, imploring him to take it, Rose said, "At least we can follow them now. *If* we get a move on, that is."

Flynn took her hand.

They walked through the long grass and up the next small hill before another expanse of meadow opened up in front of them. Flynn gasped. Another expanse of meadow and the town. It looked twice the size of the one with the rats in it. Where the town close to Home had one large tower block, this one had what looked to be hundreds. Each one stood craggy and in disrepair like most buildings in the world. Each one looked like a bony and broken finger pointing accusation at the sky, cursing it for the ruin it had brought upon them.

Despite looking across the meadow, Flynn couldn't see much more than the swaying grass. "Where have they gone?"

Rose shook her head, frowning into the strong wind. "They must have ridden off quickly."

To think of the pregnant woman and her partner being dragged behind the horses sent a kick through both Flynn's heart and stomach. "My god," he said, "they wouldn't have lasted five minutes at that pace."

Flynn looked up at the wreck of the town again. A more modern town than the one near Home, the layout seemed to be better planned. Almost as if it had been built for the world it had existed in, rather than patched together in an attempt to keep up with the changing times. The roads ran through it in a grid like the American cities he'd seen in books. They'd had a huge library in Home, including a large section of travel books, at his disposal. In his mind, he'd travelled the world several times over.

"It's going to be hard finding them in there," Rose said as she squinted against the wind.

The thought of going into the place chipped away at Flynn's courage, so he looked up at the sky to change where he focused. The clouds blocking the sun had turned gunmetal grey and the wind had grown teeth. Rain was on its way. Gooseflesh ran along both of his exposed arms. Not that he could do anything to warm up. Clothes weren't something he'd be likely to find lying around any time soon. He looked at Rose; her tiny, ripped T-shirt did little to protect her against the elements. "Did you ever come to this town when you were in your old community?"

Rose shook her head and swept her hair away from her

face, holding it in place with her hand. "No. We only really left when we wanted to hunt. We tended to stay away from civilisation. Or, rather, what had once been civilisation. I heard people had gone to the town before I joined the community, but no one went afterwards."

"What did they say of it? Anything useful?"

Rose paused for a moment before she said, "They never came back."

No time to process it, Flynn suddenly saw the Queen and her guards appear in the meadow in front of them. A dip in the landscape had hidden them from view. He grabbed Rose's shoulder and said, "Get down," as he pulled her into the long grass.

"Well," Flynn said when they were both crouched out of sight, "it's good for their prisoners that they didn't canter off."

"But bad for us," Rose replied.

"Right. I guess we've got a bit of a wait before we can follow them."

Rose shrugged and sat down next to him. "Hopefully they didn't see us."

CHAPTER 25

⨳

They waited for about twenty more minutes. The Queen and her guards had quite a distance to travel to get into the town.

While they sat on the bumpy ground, Flynn and Rose did what they seemed to do naturally whenever they waited somewhere together; they pressed close to one another, finding comfort where words didn't cut it.

So little clothes on because the Queen had only given them joggers and T-shirts, Flynn's heart beat faster to feel Rose's exposed skin against his.

The grey clouds had burst above them about ten minutes previously. Cold and wet, Flynn looked up and opened his mouth wide like he'd done several times already. It took the edge off his thirst, lubricating the cloying dryness in his throat.

"I think we can move on now," Rose said, her blonde hair darkened with the rain.

Although Flynn had been feeling that way too, he hadn't said it. If he had a choice, he'd stay there much longer with

Rose. But they needed to keep going. They could rest when they were done.

To see the wreck of the town again when he stood up—the tall dilapidated buildings against the now almost black sky—snapped a shiver through Flynn. A snort of a laugh and he shook his head. "Jeez, I thought it looked hostile *before* we sat down."

Rose didn't reply, but from the tight pull of her lips, she looked to be feeling the same anxiety as him. He watched her scan the meadow, the long grass yielding to the now stronger wind.

"Do you think we're safe to follow them now?" Flynn said.

"I dunno. I'm not sure *safe* is a good word at any time in this world."

A fair point, they'd just have to give it a try. "Okay." Flynn reached across and held his hand out to Rose. "You ready for this?" A fearful pang ran through him in case she rejected him. But she reached across and grabbed his hand, holding it in a reassuring grip.

Rose then said, "No, I'm not ready."

"I don't suppose you are. But we're as ready as we can be, right?"

A sharp nod and they stepped forward together, starting off down the hill through the long sodden grass.

CHAPTER 26

Since Flynn had seen the cuts on his wrists, they hadn't hurt anywhere near as much. The bandages were as soaked as the rest of him and pressed cold relief against the superficial cuts.

Like Flynn's T-shirt did, Rose's crop top clung to her. But he kept his eyes ahead, fighting the urge to look at how it hugged her lithe form. Every time he glanced across at her, he stared into her eyes even though she didn't always look back into his. Instead, she put most of her attention on the town in front of them and the wide road they currently walked down.

The rain fell heavier than ever, hitting the hard asphalt and bouncing back up again. It seemed that nature had a trickier time taking over the cities, and although cracked with tufts of grass sprouting through, the road still provided a smooth surface to walk down. It felt almost unnatural to not have to accommodate the peaks and divots of a lumpy meadow.

Unlike the town with the rats, this town had a wide highway leading into it. No narrow railway bridge to walk beneath. They could have walked down the centre, but Flynn and Rose kept to the edge of it—the grass long on either side—just in case they needed to hide in a hurry.

A metal footbridge crossed over the road. At first it had been hard to see, but the closer they got, the easier it became for Flynn to work out exactly what hung from it. As much as he wanted to look away, he forced himself not to. It was important he acknowledged it.

It took for Rose to vocalise what they saw. "Do you think it's the man she dragged here?"

Flynn didn't answer. He didn't need to. The bloody corpse had been strung up by his neck. Bound hands behind his back and bound ankles, his face showed the stress of his entire body weight on his throat. Completely naked, he was covered in sores. Grass and dirt stuck to his exposed and fresh wounds.

"What do you think's happened to the pregnant woman?" Flynn said.

"We couldn't have done anything, you know," Rose replied.

"I could have let you run after them."

"But the Queen was just over the hill. If they'd made any kind of fuss, which I would have expected them to—especially because I would have run at them—we would have been captured with them."

Flynn opened his mouth to reply, but Rose cut him off. "And then once the Queen had them, if we'd exposed ourselves at that point, they would have killed us instantly. We couldn't risk our lives for two people. Not when we have so many others depending on us. We had to make a decision for the greater good at that point."

"I just can't help thinking I made a bad call when I told you to wait."

Rose grabbed both of Flynn's hands in hers. "You saved

us both with that call. I was thinking with my heart. *You* used your head."

"And killed them."

"You didn't kill them, Flynn."

Both Flynn and Rose stopped when they were nearly beneath the bridge and looked up at the man again. His rope creaked as he swayed in the strong wind. The rain smashed against his exposed skin. "It's just so hard to look at this."

"I know. But we did what we had to do. Knowing what I know now, I would have made the call you did. By the time we had a chance to help them, it was already too late. We'd be hanging with him if it had gone any other way."

It all made sense, but it didn't take away any of the guilt. Flynn walked to the side of the bridge and stepped onto the bottom step leading up it.

"What are you doing?" Rose said.

"I'm going to cut him down. It's the least we can do."

"And let the Queen know someone's in the town? Someone hostile to her and her actions."

"We can't leave him up there, Rose."

"Of course we can. What use is a dead body to us? What are we going to do with him?"

A look from the hanging man and back to Rose again, Flynn said, "He deserves better than this."

"Yes, he *did.* But he's dead now. He isn't that lump of meat up there. He's gone."

She had a point.

"Look," Rose said, "we have a choice. We can cut him down, but if we do, we have to then get out of here. I'm not going to show the Queen we've been here and then go looking around. It's risky enough as it is."

"The Queen might think someone else has cut him down. I dunno, nomads or something."

"Nomads would eat him."

Flynn shrugged.

"Okay, let's say she doesn't work out it's us. Either way, it'll put her on high alert. I'd rather catch her with her pants down. I don't know this city at all, I don't want anything making it harder for us. If we leave him there, we might still be able to save his pregnant partner."

And what could Flynn say to that?

"Come on," Rose said and pointed at the town. "Let's get off this road and hide somewhere in there." She looked around. "I feel vulnerable out here. We can do so much more if the Queen doesn't know we're coming."

When Rose set off again, walking beneath the footbridge in the direction of the town, Flynn paused for a second and watched the dead man swing. The horror of his violent end sat in his wide eyes and protruding tongue. "I'm sorry," he said to him. "I'm sorry I failed you." He stepped off the bridge and ran after Rose.

CHAPTER 27

⚜

Flynn and Rose arrived at the first building in the town without incident. Like most buildings in most towns, it used to be an office block. Vicky had told Flynn the old world didn't give people many career choices beyond a cubicle existence.

Flynn scanned all the glassless windows of the large buildings on either side of the main street. Darkness sat inside. And maybe people, but he couldn't see them if they did. If he'd had anything to do with securing this town for use, he'd have guards watching the main road at all times. Hopefully the Queen hadn't thought of that. Or, at the very least, hopefully she felt confident enough that she didn't worry.

"Any ideas where the shit slope is?" Flynn said. "We find that and we've found the dungeon."

Before Rose could respond, the clop of several horses echoed through the town. They got rapidly louder as they drew closer, their hooves hammering against the asphalt.

Rose jumped through the ground-floor window of the

office block next to them and Flynn followed her a second later.

Both Flynn and Rose dropped down and pressed their backs against the wall beneath the window. They listened to the thunder of hooves race past them outside. They were heading in the direction of the wide exit road.

When it had quieted down, Flynn said, "Do you think that was all of them leaving?"

Rose shook her head. "No. It would have been much louder if it was all of them."

"What shall we do?"

"Stay in these buildings," Rose said. "If we move through them, we should remain hidden. There's enough of them for us to stay in the shadows for as long as we need to."

Flynn followed Rose through the ground floor of the office block. Every time they passed another glassless window, he checked outside. It seemed clear. Other than the wind, nothing moved through the streets.

Rose stopped and chewed the inside of her mouth as she looked around.

Flynn came to a halt next to her, trying to work out what she'd seen. "Do you think there's another group of people in here? Other than the Queen and her lot."

After she'd moved off and snaked through several smashed desks and toppled chairs, Rose stopped again and whispered back, "I don't know. Why would there be?"

"The Queen said she left the bodies of the people who died during the games for the people who ran this town."

"Hmm, maybe, then. I think we need to assume there's someone around every corner, Queen's gang or not. It's the only way to remain vigilant enough to get through this."

The rain had stopped, but a strong breeze still raced through the holes in the building. It kicked up a snowstorm of styrofoam from where several ceiling tiles had fallen out and shattered on the ground. Still soaked from the rain, Flynn shivered. So much for summertime.

At the other side of the first building, Rose vaulted through the downstairs window into an alleyway beyond. She landed with the slightest of sounds.

When Flynn followed her out, the slap of his feet against the hard ground clapped away from him in both directions. He looked at Rose while wincing a silent apology.

For the next few seconds, Flynn held his breath as they both waited. The wind stung his sore eyes, but he refused to blink while he searched for people around them.

"Come on," Rose finally whispered, and she climbed through the next window into the next office.

The sound of the wind remained a constant. As did the lack of any other noise. Hopefully no one had heard him. He climbed through the empty window after Rose.

Rose set off again and Flynn walked beside her. He continued to look around, remaining as alert as he could to any sounds outside. The office building looked like every other office building he'd been in. Cheap furniture broken and overturned. Cracked computer monitors. Styrofoam ceiling tiles, half of them missing and smashed into little pieces, gathered in the corners of the rooms as tiny white balls. His dad had told him how boring his life used to be and had joked about how he enjoyed his existence more with scores of diseased in the world. It meant he got to spend every day with his son. A flash of his dad getting dragged into the water made Flynn flinch. When he snapped out of it, he saw Rose had pulled ahead of him. He jogged to catch up with her.

Outside the next office block, Flynn and Rose paused again to listen. Still nothing other than the wind. They were standing next to what used to be a pub. Vicky had told Flynn all about them. Apparently when people weren't in offices, they were in pubs, getting drunk. Very little alcohol existed in the world now. The occasional spirit and bottle of wine still left over, but not much else.

The pub smelled of dust. So much wood in the place, it also reeked of rot. The funk of decay in most buildings suggested they were one strong gust away from collapse. Although, amongst all the ruin, Flynn saw a bar that ran along one wall and still shone with the varnish of years ago. It had a matte look to it because of the sheer amount of dust, but it was only one wipe away from looking as good as new.

The small amount of remaining carpet squelched beneath Flynn's steps, each squish aggravating a smell of stagnant water. The areas by the windows had none left at all. No doubt years of soakings had chewed away at it, leaving small patches scattered across the concrete floor like scabs.

Much like the offices, the pub had broken tables and turned-over chairs. It gave an impression of an existence in the old world that was sedentary to the point of stagnation. Flynn spoke to Rose in a whisper. "Vicky told me that cigarettes and alcohol ran out before food did. Apparently people were more concerned with getting pissed than they were with eating."

"I don't suppose many people expected to live that long. Better to be drunk when the diseased chow down on you than sober."

"Did any of the communities you were in have alcohol?"

"No," Rose whispered back.

"Brian wanted to start brewing some even though Serj was always against the idea. He said tensions ran high enough without complicating things with booze. I'd imagine Brian's probably started his own brewery now."

Rose didn't reply. Instead, she exited the pub. Flynn returned to looking around as he followed her. The area outside still looked clear.

They entered another office building that sat next to the pub. Another useless, tall block filled with broken desks and chairs.

They'd walked about halfway across the ground floor when a loud *thud* sounded above them. Flynn pulled in a sharp breath and froze. A look at Rose and he saw her with her mouth wide as she stared up at the ceiling.

Suddenly a rush of footsteps ran through the building. The ceiling shook like it could collapse. *Fuck!* Rose mouthed.

Flynn looked around and saw a cupboard. The door had been ripped off, but with no light in there, they could probably hide out in it. They didn't have many choices. When the thuds hit what sounded like stairs leading down to them, he grabbed Rose's arm and dragged her over to it.

CHAPTER 28

As Flynn and Rose huddled in the darkness of the cupboard, they listened to the footsteps from the floor above run down the stairs. The slap of feet against metal rang through the building. It sounded like at least ten people heading their way.

To get himself as deep into the shadows as he could, Flynn pushed against the wall and pulled Rose back with him.

The cupboard's lack of windows left it poorly ventilated, the reek of dust so thick in the air Flynn could taste it. He ruffled his nose against its stench.

When a voice called through the building, Flynn felt Rose jump next to him and his pulse spiked.

"Stay there!" it said. It sounded like the Queen.

The sound of the Queen's footsteps stomped towards them and Flynn pushed against the wall. Not that it would get him any farther away from her.

Flynn balled his fists to get ready to fight. It didn't matter how many guards she had with her, he wouldn't go down easily, and he'd make sure he took her down with him.

When the Queen appeared in front of the cupboard, Flynn's heart kicked and the breath left his lungs. He felt Rose press into him to get away from her.

A deep scowl on her angular face, the Queen stopped in plain sight. But she didn't look at them. Maybe she didn't know they were there. Although, they couldn't surprise attack her now. Too many guards waited out of sight.

Wide-eyed as if driven by mania, the Queen looked to be in a hurry as she re-righted one of the toppled desks. She then pulled down her tight-fitting trousers and knickers, and bent over it, pointing her bare arse out behind her.

"What the fuck?" Rose whispered.

As repulsive as he found the woman, Flynn couldn't look away.

A second set of footsteps walked over to the Queen. When Flynn saw him come into view, he assumed he was her new toy boy. Younger than Flynn by a few years, but probably in his twenties, he had a pale complexion and looked nervous. He didn't need telling to pull his trousers down, his penis hanging limp when he'd freed it. No wonder he looked scared. She'd rip the fucking thing off if he didn't perform.

"What are you waiting for?" the Queen barked as she looked over her shoulder at him.

Thank god Flynn had avoided that.

The boy shook and stammered, "Um … um …"

"Don't fucking 'um' me. *Fuck* me, you useless prick!"

The boy grabbed a hold of himself and massaged his penis. He stared down at it as if offended by the way his body had betrayed him.

"I'll heal up if you don't fucking hurry!"

The boy walked close to her, whimpering as he tried to enter her.

"What's fucking wrong with you?" the Queen said. After standing up, she grabbed his cock and the boy gasped.

As painful as it looked, it seemed to do the trick.

The Queen bent over again. The boy had better luck the second time.

∾

ONLY ABOUT TWO MINUTES PASSED WHILE FLYNN AND ROSE watched the Queen and her victim. The desire to run out and kill her burned within Flynn. Something about not being able to see the guards had him thinking he could do it. That he could rescue her latest prisoner. Like a child when they closed their eyes and thought they were hiding; if he couldn't see the guards, they weren't there. But they were and he needed to keep his head.

A loud gasp rushed through the office and the boy quickly pulled out of the Queen. He grabbed a hold of his penis, pushed her top up to expose her bare back, and ejaculated over it. The strength seemed to leave him as he fell on top of her, panting with his release.

Not that the Queen stood there for long. In one fluid movement, she spun around, threw the boy off her, pulled a knife from her belt, and pressed it against his throat.

His semi-flaccid penis hanging down, the boy snapped board stiff and stared at her. The colour had returned to his face from the few minutes of exertion.

"What the fuck was that, boy?" the Queen said to him.

A warble ran through his words. "I'm sorry, it was too quick."

"It was fucking quick, but that's *not* what I'm talking about."

"What?" The boy gasped, a frown crushing his face.

"You came on my back."

"That's what we're supposed to do. I didn't want you to get …" The sound of the wind ran through the office for a few seconds, highlighting the silence left by the boy.

"Guards!" the Queen shrieked, so loud it echoed out into the streets beyond.

The thunder of footsteps ran into the place and several royal blue guards appeared in front of Flynn and Rose. Did the Queen know they were there? Was this one of her twisted games where she suddenly revealed that she knew she had an audience?

"Take him to the plaza," the Queen said, her voice already calmer than before.

One of the guards took the Queen's blade from her and kept it pressed to the boy's throat. She stared straight at him and spoke in a low voice. "Walk. Now!"

Trousers around his ankles still, the boy tried to shuffle away.

"Pull your fucking trousers up, you moron," the guard said to him.

Once the boy had pulled his trousers up, the guard led him away.

When all of the guards and the Queen had gone from their view, Flynn heard Rose release a quiet sigh.

CHAPTER 29

Rose moved with far more grace and stealth than Flynn, so he let her lead the way as they followed the Queen, her victim, and her band of bitches from the office block.

What Flynn had just witnessed had made his head spin, so he needed Rose to do the thinking for both of them at that moment. He'd been in the situation the boy was now in, but he hadn't quite put it together as rape. In his ignorance, he'd not thought a woman could do that to a man. But now he'd seen it happen—and seeing the tormented state of the poor boy afterwards—gave him a new perspective.

They had waited about thirty seconds before emerging from the cupboard. If the Queen had known they were there, she surely would have set a trap for when they came out, but they hadn't met any resistance so far.

The party walked at a fast march, so Flynn and Rose had to move at a similar pace to keep up. They hung back far enough to be out of sight, the group ahead creating enough noise to make them easy to follow. Mostly heavy footsteps, he also heard the occasional wail from the young man. God knew what they were doing to him. Or what they planned to do to him.

At the front of the office block, Rose peered out into the abandoned street. She then pulled back and stood aside so Flynn could do the same. He saw the group walking down the middle of the road, taking a path that led them deeper into the town.

If Flynn and Rose followed them directly, they'd make themselves far too easy to spot. Instead, they moved through the shadows, only exposing themselves as they slipped out of the office building into the shop next to it.

A long line of shops stretched ahead of them. Each large display window had already been smashed with no sign of ever being there. It meant there wouldn't be any glass to give them away by popping beneath their steps.

Many of the boy toy's screams were indecipherable to Flynn when he'd been farther away, but as they got closer—the shops offering the perfect cover so they could move nearer to the gang—he heard him more clearly.

"Please," the boy said, twisting against the tight grip one of the royal guards had on him. "I didn't mean to. I didn't think. Please!"

They got to the point where the crowd in front were only a few metres ahead, so they waited where they were, the strong wind rushing into the empty shop and blasting them with the grit and dust it picked up from the ground.

Both Flynn and Rose watched the Queen and her crew disappear down an alleyway between an old hotel and more shops.

The large abandoned hotel cast a long shadow. The office blocks were one thing, but something about hotels, hospitals, and other twenty-four-hour buildings gave Flynn the creeps. He could barely remember a time when they were operational, but even the look of them showed him they were places that were designed to always be busy. They now stood utterly silent, a ghost of what they once were.

Although the obvious move, it didn't make Flynn feel any less apprehensive to watch Rose burst from the shelter of the shop they were in and sprint out into the road in the direction of the huge building. A weary sigh, he fell forwards into a jog as he followed after her.

∿

THE VAST, HIGH-CEILINGED FOYER HAD THE SAME SMELL OF dust and mould that every other building had. The large wooden desk at the front stood as resilient as the bar they'd seen in the pub. A layer of dust coated its glossy surface, dulling its shine.

On one side of the foyer, Flynn saw two large metal doors. Once elevators, they now stood as rusty wrecks, a slight parting down the middle of them from where they could no longer hold their form. The red of their decay bled into the off-white walls surrounding them.

Rose moved through the space on her tiptoes. When Flynn followed, his footsteps were the only ones to make a noise. She had the flight of an assassin. Him, the flight of a hippo.

A few seconds later, Rose disappeared from sight as she ducked through a doorless entry leading to the rooms on the ground floor.

The dirty brown and red carpet might have muted Flynn's footsteps when he followed her, but the smell of it rotting hung heavily like it had at the pub. The reek of decomposition filled the air, so thick it damn near stuck to Flynn's sweating skin. Also, like in the pub, large patches of carpet had been eaten away beneath the smashed windows. Those spots had clearly borne the brunt of the elements over the years. How long would it take for nature to conquer the entire synthetic monstrosity? Or maybe the hotel would collapse before the carpet vanished. Either way, the slow chew of entropy would turn everything to dust eventually.

Were he not trying to keep the noise down, Flynn would have asked Rose if she'd been there before. She moved through the hotel like she knew the way. Greyhound quick, he had to fight to keep up with her.

Rose turned a sharp left and Flynn followed her. Although he saw the dead end in front of them, she hadn't turned around, so he didn't either.

Doors leading to old guest rooms lined either side of the corridor. Hopefully they were empty. The group they followed with the Queen and the man had far fewer people in it than rode into the town. In such a big place, they couldn't even begin to guess where the others were.

A window frame at the end of the corridor looked small enough for them to peer out of and still remain hidden in the dark shadows a step back from it. Hopefully it would give them some kind of insight as to what the Queen planned to do with the boy and where she kept her prisoners.

Rose had already looked out and watched Flynn when he caught up to her. He copied her, remaining in the shadows as he stared through the empty window frame. He gasped at what he saw: a large, open, cobblestone plaza. The memories of restaurants and cafes still clung to the crumbling wrecks around the space. A fierce bonfire burned in the middle with an empty spit over it. But worst of all, he saw the pregnant woman they should have saved.

A group of hunters were there, holding onto her, but the Queen and her bitches weren't. At least they'd found a large part of the Queen's party and some of the others had already left the town. Hopefully the rest stood in front of them at that moment; they didn't need any nasty surprises hiding in the shadows.

When Flynn pulled back from the window and looked at Rose, she glared at him. It seemed clear what she meant by her look. It said *shut the fuck up and don't do anything stupid.*

But he couldn't ignore the pregnant woman, still bound by her wrists and under the watchful eye of several guards. He'd failed her once; could he really do it again? Her boyfriend had died because of Flynn's cowardice. If they could save her this time, maybe it would somehow make up for his earlier failings.

Flynn looked back at Rose to see her stare at him like she'd swing for him. And he agreed with her, he really did. It would be madness, hell, it would be fucking suicide to help the woman. But would his conscience let him walk away a second time?

CHAPTER 30

It took for Flynn to look out of the window again to see one of the hunters had a knife pressed against the pregnant woman's throat. As she stood there, she bit on her bottom lip as if fighting against her desire to cry out. What would have started as a pilgrimage to somewhere safer than where they'd been had turned into her being dragged behind a horse, witnessing her lover's murder, and now facing death at the hands of one of the Queen's lackeys. All with only a few days left before she gave birth.

Still soaked from the rain, the woman's top hugged her huge bulge. Surely Flynn owed it to her and her unborn child to help them. Another glance at Rose and she still stared at him. It felt like she could read his thoughts.

Flynn looked away from the woman and he suddenly saw it. A hole had been hacked into the ground in the plaza. A large hole, large enough to drop an entire car into. It had a rusty grate over the top of it. The grate had been bolted shut. The hole had been filled with water, and along the grate's bars were the clasped hands of at least ten people. It looked like ten women from what he could see.

The desire to help the woman ebbed away at the sight of it. Flynn's pulse ran to the edge of a panic attack. If he ended up in there, he'd drown.

Several deep breaths helped blunt the claws of his anxiety. Flynn didn't have to step out of the hotel. At present, they were hidden well enough from the guards. He wouldn't end up in that pit unless he chose to reveal himself.

The sound of the Queen's voice made Flynn jump. It ran through the plaza, but he couldn't yet see her. "Put her back!"

The hunter with the pregnant woman kept the knife to her throat and looked in the direction of the sound. "Huh?"

"Are you fucking deaf? I *said* put her back."

The hunter looked like he wanted to question it again and Flynn silently willed him to do so. Give the Queen someone to focus her fury on rather than the woman. But he clearly had the good sense to keep his mouth shut. He walked over to the pit and dragged the pregnant woman with him. The crack of the bolt snapped through the plaza, followed by the groan of the large hinges as he lifted the grate up.

The exhausted faces of all the women in the pool looked up at the guard. Some of them looked close to giving up, their eyes half closed with fatigue. How many lay at the bottom already?

The hunter waved his knife at the pregnant woman and she climbed into the pool.

Just watching someone plunge into water made Flynn's stomach lurch. But at least they had more time to rescue her. He wouldn't give up on her. He owed her.

The hunter let go of the grate and it crashed back into place. The jangly sound of it played with Flynn's already frayed nerves and a gentle shake trembled through him.

Suddenly the Queen came into view, twisting Flynn's anxiety up another notch. They were so close to her, but if they remained where they were, she wouldn't be able to see them. The darkness of their corridor gave them enough shadow to hide in and still watch.

The Queen then pulled away the knife she held to the man's throat and shoved him towards one of her hunters. She stared at him as she said, "We're going to cook *him* today."

"Please," the boy said as he twisted against the hunter's grip. "I didn't realise."

"Well, you're an idiot, then," the Queen said. "Either way, I don't want you near me."

"But—"

Before he could say anything else, the Queen stepped towards him and cut his throat.

The speed of it forced Flynn back a step. His pulse quickened as he watched a red line spread across his neck, blood quickly gushing out of it.

To watch it turned the back of Flynn's knees weak. He had to lean against the wall to remain upright. He looked at Rose and saw she'd turned pale too.

The man fell to the ground in a dead heap. The Queen stood over his corpse for a second, a tight grip on her knife, blood dripping from its shiny blade. "Spit-roast the cunt," she said.

Several hunters rushed over and dragged the corpse away.

CHAPTER 31

Although already standing back from the window so as to remain hidden in the corridor's shadows, Flynn pulled even farther back after the Queen had killed the young man. He leaned against the crumbling wall and stared at his feet. Having already seen too much, he wanted to avoid any more of the brutality. Especially as he could do nothing to stop it at that time.

A few seconds later, Rose moved to be next to him. She'd clearly reached the same conclusion.

They might have stepped far enough back not to be able to see outside anymore, but they still heard everything.

"Do you want him skinned?" one of the hunters asked.

Despite everything he'd been through and seen over the years, the question still turned Flynn's stomach. Bad enough skinning a rabbit, it must have been brutal to do it to a human.

"No," the Queen replied, the silence hanging for a moment before she added, "I like the crackling."

Flynn relied on the wall more than before, letting his exhausted body press against it, parts of it puffy from where the plaster had swollen and burst. An urge to sit down tugged on him, but if he did that, he might not get back up again.

A deep inhale and he listened to the sound of what must have been the body being dragged over the concrete. How could they leave the pregnant woman out there with that lot? Although, how could they not leave her? There was no fucking way he'd risk getting thrown in that damn water pit. And even if he did feel brave enough to face the water, he and Rose had no chance against the army outside.

A soft touch from Rose pulled Flynn out of his thoughts. When he looked at her, she said, "We can't help her at the moment. We wouldn't last two seconds out there."

The hunters huffed and puffed as they clearly prepared the body. Several slaps of flesh against stone before a wet squelch came through the window at them. Flynn's stomach turned over on itself to listen to what must have been the spit going in hard and fast.

The sounds died down outside and Flynn's nausea eased slightly. "I'm guessing this town belongs to the Queen," he whispered.

So close to Flynn their shoulders were touching, Rose looked at him and said, "Huh?"

"Well, she made a big deal at the games about leaving the bodies as an offering for the people who run this town. From what we've just seen, I'm guessing the people who run this town are her and her guards."

After nodding at him, a detached glaze in her eyes, Rose said, "It seems that way, doesn't it? That's probably why they look so much healthier than the other people in the royal complex."

"All the protein?"

"Right. I'm sure if you can accept the trauma of it, it's probably quite nutritious."

Flynn felt colder than before and shivered. "Although, to look into their sunken eyes, I'm not sure they have accepted it. Eating another person has to come with consequences."

A female voice ran through the plaza outside. "When will we attack Home?"

The Queen replied, her sharp tones now so recognisable to Flynn, he had a Pavlovian response to them, the flesh along his spine pulling tight. "I want a *feast* before we go."

"So when's the next games?" The royal guards seemed to be in that privileged position where they could ask the Queen questions without fear of reprimand.

"We have twelve people in the dungeon. It won't be long before a few more idiots follow the signs into our spider's web. We would have had two more were that bitch not pregnant and were her partner not a fool. We'll do the games, cram all the events into one day to speed everything up, and then make our move."

Flynn moved farther away from the window and Rose followed him. "I can't believe we didn't see it before," he said. "The games are just a ruse. It's not about giving one person a chance—"

"It's about giving a group of people a feast," Rose finished for him.

A deep breath filled Flynn's lungs with the dusty decay of the hotel. "We need to put an end to this."

"Besides," the Queen said, her voice quieter for the distance Flynn and Rose had put between them, "those two lovebirds would have gone straight back to Home when they escaped. They'll be expecting us if we go too soon. We need to give it time. Home's been there for years, another few days won't hurt."

To hear the Queen talk about them directly sent an anxious spike through Flynn. When he looked at Rose, she raised her eyebrows at him. He said, "She's not forgotten about us, then?"

"I'm not sure she will," Rose said.

To think of the watery pit sped Flynn's breaths up. "We need to take her down. We need to take her down before she takes us down."

"And how are we going to do that?"

Flynn now turned his back on the window and walked down the corridor. He turned right at the end, heading towards the foyer with Rose beside him. "We need an army formidable enough to know we have a good chance of defeating her."

They entered the foyer, the acoustics in the large space catching their steps and amplifying them. Hopefully no one heard them.

"And you have one, do you?" Rose asked. "Because twelve prisoners who may or may not want to fight won't cut it."

"No, they won't. But I've got a plan."

CHAPTER 32

No matter how tightly wound he felt, a walk always helped Flynn relax. Whenever he filled his lungs with the fresh breeze, it helped calm him down. When things had been too much for him in Home, he'd find a reason to go on a scavenging mission. Just being away from the stress of the place and out in the open did something to settle his soul. Unfortunately, the problems were always still there when he returned.

About three hours had passed since they'd left the Queen's town. They'd walked through the July heat, the rain clouds and chill having been burned away by the persistence of the summer sun. Flynn had gone from feeling cold to being covered in an itchy layer of sweat.

For the first time in what felt like forever, they didn't run into any trouble on their walk. No nomads, hunters, or any other reason to duck into a hostile town. The gods had obviously decided they'd already seen enough that day—maybe they knew something about what they were walking into.

For most of their journey, Flynn and Rose held hands. Even when the contact of their palms got sweaty, neither let go—a strong reassurance that they were there for one another. They were walking into the unknown, and it could go awfully wrong. But Rose had promised she would let Flynn handle it. It was his trial to face alone.

They reached the same spot he'd been in with the Queen a few days ago, and Flynn looked down over the large complex. A part of his attention on his breathing, he tried to remain calm and banish the butterflies in his stomach. It didn't work.

Flynn glanced at the strong wooden fence surrounding the place, the complex network of tubes and pipes to collect rainwater, and the small mound that looked like nothing from a distance, but hid over one hundred bedrooms beneath it.

When Flynn looked at the wooden structure in the middle of Home, his composure slipped and he drew a deep breath to try to rein it in. "It all started with the need to get lead for that barn." He swallowed against the grief rising in his throat. "Were it not for that, Serj wouldn't have died and I wouldn't have found out all the things I did. I wouldn't feel obliged to help because I'd still be ignorant about the Queen and her vile existence. And maybe she wouldn't have turned her attention on Home."

A squeeze of his hand and Rose smiled at him, her vulnerability evident in the crooked twist of uncertainty. "But we wouldn't have met one another."

It loosened some of the tension in Flynn. And Angelica would have still finished it with him. Rather than having an excuse to leave, he would have had to stand by and watch her and Larry swan around together. "I wouldn't change meeting you for the world," he said to Rose. "Even knowing what I had to go through to get to this point."

Rose's mouth opened ever so slightly as she stared at him. He inched a step closer to her. Should he try to kiss her again? Although she stood there, not pulling away, she also hadn't stepped forward. What if she rejected him again?

The moment lasted too long. Rose turned away from him and looked at Home. "What do you think they're going to say to you?"

A weary sigh and Flynn shook his head at himself. Another opportunity missed. She'd already made it clear how she felt; he didn't need to be afraid of her rejection anymore. He tugged Rose with him as he started down the hill towards the place. "I really don't know. I can't expect they'll welcome me with open arms, but they're not bad people. They may be arseholes and fools, but they're not evil. They have a moral compass and they abide by it. They killed Vicky because they blamed her for the state of the world."

"Do you think they had a point?"

Another deep sigh and Flynn shrugged. "You obviously do."

Before Rose could reply, Flynn quickly said, "I'm sorry. I didn't mean that." He then added, "I can see why they did what they did, but they *killed* Vicky."

Rose didn't respond and she let go of his hand. He might have apologised, but he couldn't take back the hurt he'd clearly just inflicted on her with his snappy response.

CHAPTER 33

When they were no more than twenty metres from the gates, they stopped. Hard to tell who, but one of the guards on watch stood up from their post and shielded their eyes as they looked over at Flynn and Rose. Suddenly the reality of what they were walking into hit Flynn, his nerves buzzing with electric anxiety. He broke the silence between them. "You have to let this play out however it needs to happen, okay?"

"What if they try to kill you?" Rose said.

"They won't."

"You know that for sure?"

"No, but I'm pretty confident it'll be okay. Besides, we've got to trust everything will work out, right? My intention is good, that's all I have."

Rose didn't reply.

The large gates shook for a second before one of them opened wide enough to let someone out. It took a few moments before Flynn recognised the man. "Dan," he said.

Rose spoke to him from the side of her mouth. "One of the ones you tied up?"

"Yep."

"Oh fuck."

"Yep." When Flynn felt Rose tense beside him, he added, "Don't get involved. He needs to do whatever he's about to do."

She didn't reply.

"I need you to promise me, Rose. I don't want you to get involved."

Although Flynn kept his attention on Dan, he had an awareness of Rose's frame loosening. Again, she didn't reply.

Dan marched towards Flynn and Rose through the long grass, his arms swinging, his feet stamping down with his purposeful gait. "You! What the *fuck* are you doing back here?"

But Flynn didn't respond.

A look from Flynn to Dan, and Rose said, "Why aren't you telling him?"

"He won't listen at the moment. He needs to vent first before he hears anything I have to say. He needs to tell me how much of an arsehole I am."

Dan continued towards them. Tension coiled through his frame and he had a baton strapped to his hip, but he hadn't pulled it out yet. That had to be a good sign.

Now only about five metres away, Flynn felt Rose's tension wind up another notch. "Everything will be okay. Don't put yourself in harm's way by trying to help me. You have to trust me on this. They'll listen eventually and you'll only make it worse if you get involved."

"I don't like it. It feels like suicide."

"They won't kill me. They're not like that. They may be many things, but they don't kill unless they feel like they have to." Flynn raised his hands above his head in surrender. "I'm no threat to them at the moment."

Now he'd gotten much closer, the swish of the long grass accompanied Dan's march. Red-faced and twisted with rage, he stared at Flynn as if Rose didn't exist.

As much as Flynn wanted to raise his guard, he kept his arms in the air and stared at Dan. The words sat on the edge of his tongue. They were there to save them. To give them a heads-up about the Queen. But he could tell Dan wouldn't listen to him. Not yet.

Just a metre between them, Flynn smiled as he said, "Hi, Dan."

A flash of light crashed into Flynn's left cheek. It sent tendrils of fiery pain through his face. But it didn't knock him out.

Flynn blinked against watering eyes and smiled again. "Is that all you've got?"

The second blow connected with Flynn's temple and his world turned dark.

CHAPTER 34

Hard to tell exactly how long had passed because Flynn had been unconscious for a time before he came round. Maybe a day, maybe longer. When he first woke up, he thought he'd lost his sight. The bruising on his left cheek and temple hurt as a dull throb. Although when he became fully conscious, he realised he'd been locked in one of Home's dark rooms. No electricity anymore, if they wanted to lock him up, the room would inevitably be pitch black. They certainly wouldn't leave a prisoner with lit candles.

They'd dressed him in fresh clothes. That much he felt. A sweatshirt and joggers, the clean softness of them lay against his skin. The bandages around his wrists had also gone and his cuts felt much better. They were coated with hard scabs, but they didn't hurt like they had.

Flynn then heard sounds outside. A second later, the light from the hallway flooded in and he covered his eyes against the blinding sting of it.

Brian walked in first, Sharon and Dan coming in behind him. They could have brought candles; instead they left the door open so the natural light out in the hallway illuminated the room. Dan remained close to the door. It showed Flynn that he shouldn't consider running out of there. Not that he had.

"Well, well, well," the bearded man said, a smug grin on his round face.

"Is that all you've got?" Flynn asked.

Brian turned serious and scowled at him.

"You sound like a bad villain from one of those awful action movies Serj would make me watch. Next you'll produce a white cat and start stroking it slowly as you stare at me."

It seemed to take Brian's words from him. He produced a knife easily as long as the one Flynn had used on him. The smile returned. "Bet you'd rather a monologue now, eh?"

Flynn didn't reply. Even he knew when to shut the fuck up.

"So you found the bed, I see?"

Sharon and Dan sniggered and Flynn looked from one to the other and back to Brian again. What had they done to it? He held back his reply. Whatever they'd done, they didn't deserve a reaction.

A look around the room, his hard piggy stare lingering on the bed, Brian said, "You know whose room this used to be?"

Flynn scanned the walls and the shelves. They were empty, suggesting no one stayed in there now. "How the fuck would I know? I was unconscious when you brought me here."

"Thought you might have worked it out," Sharon said. "We figured you would have been able to smell her."

"Who?" Flynn's pulse quickened. "Vicky?"

"No, you fucking moron." Brian sat down on the bed with

him, the metal frame groaning beneath his weight. He kept his knife raised in Flynn's direction. "Angelica."

"This isn't Angelica's room, you muppet."

"No." Dan spoke this time. "It's Larry's. She's been in this bed quite a few times over the past year or two."

All three of Home's guards smiled at Flynn. Smug satisfaction twisted each one of their bitter faces.

Flynn looked from Sharon to Dan and back to Brian. He stopped on Brian and stared at him for a second. A smile then crept across his face. It soon turned into a laugh.

"You think it's funny?" Brian said, his deep scowl showing he'd been rattled. "You think it's funny that Angelica cheated on you for at least a year before she found the balls to tell you? That she fucked another man on the regular."

Flynn laughed harder than before and Brian kept going. "That she probably thought about Larry when she was with you."

Where he'd been sat cross-legged on the bed, Flynn dropped his feet over the side and leaned on his knees, having to sit up because of the force of his bellowing laughs.

"What?" Brian said and pointed his knife at Flynn. "Tell me what's so fucking funny."

To stop his laughter, Flynn pressed the back of his right hand to his nose and looked at the man. "I was just thinking about how you pissed yourself when I tied you up. I knew you'd be frightened, but I never thought *that* would happen. You were like a small child."

Brian lurched forward and Dan jumped on him, pulling him back from Flynn, both of his hands gripped around Brian's right wrist to hold the knife back.

As Dan wrestled with Brian, Sharon wriggled the knife

free from him. Although Brian might have wanted Flynn dead, the other two clearly didn't.

Now Dan had Brian restrained, Flynn looked at the three guards. Where he'd laughed only moments before, his stomach tightened with his anger towards them. They'd killed Vicky. "You've had your fun," he said. "It's time to stop now. If you three push me any more, I'll make sure I cut your fucking eyes out and set you loose in the wild. I'll let this cruel world decide your fate because I've already allowed you too many concessions. Remember, I could have killed all three of you on the night I left. You're only here now because I've allowed it, against my better judgement."

"You're full of shit," Sharon said.

A look up and down the length of her body and Flynn sneered at her, "Although, if I do set you loose, I don't think you'll be good for anything but eating. Even a desperate man would have a hard time finding *you* attractive."

Red-faced and tight-lipped, Sharon pulled in a deep breath and straightened her back. But she didn't reply to him.

"So why did you come back?" Dan said, a tight grip still on Brian, who twisted occasionally as if he could break free of his restraint.

"Because Home's going to be attacked."

"What do you care?"

"If it was just you three here, then I wouldn't care at all. You three, Angelica, and Larry can go to hell. But it isn't just you, even if you do run the place like it is. There's an entire community out there. A community with children and teenagers who haven't done anything wrong."

"*We* haven't done anything wrong," Sharon said.

"You keep telling yourself that, sweetheart."

"We *haven't*!"

After drawing a weary sigh, Flynn looked at Sharon. "Do we really need to go over it again?"

"No." Dan interrupted and looked at his wife as if to tell her to leave it.

The face Sharon pulled made Flynn smirk again. Screwed up tighter than a puckered arsehole, she looked ready to blow. He then said, "He's got a tight leash on you, hasn't he?" He turned to Dan. "Can you make her do tricks?"

"Stop being a prick, Flynn, and tell us who's going to attack us."

"I'm not telling you."

"What?"

Another snap from Brian as he tried to break free, Dan restraining him again. "Just let me gut him. I don't care about this nonsense," Brian said.

But Flynn ignored him and addressed Dan. "I want to speak to the community. I want them to hear what's coming for you. I want *them* to decide their fate."

"We're not letting you talk to them."

"Worried I might tell them the truth?"

"We've got nothing to hide," Dan said. "Vicky created this mess."

Although Flynn tried to respond, Sharon cut him off. "You do realise we have your little girlfriend as leverage, right? No one knows we have her, so we can do what the fuck we like to her."

"You won't."

"Why?"

"Because, although you're complete fucking arseholes, you're principled people. You act for what you think are the right reasons. And no matter how misguided the three of you are, even you can see there isn't any reason to be mean to Rose."

Silence swept through the room, and when Brian fought again to be free of Dan's restraint, Dan let go. The bearded man walked out into the corridor, followed by Sharon a moment later.

After he'd looked at Flynn for a few more seconds, Dan shook his head and stood up. At the door, he sighed and pulled it closed. Just before he locked him in again, Flynn heard him say, "I hope you like the dark."

CHAPTER 35

Hours passed before the door opened again. As before, the light stung Flynn's eyes while he adjusted to the sudden change. He sat up on Larry's bed—the old metal frame creaking—blinked repeatedly, and rubbed his face in an attempt to speed up his recovery.

Brian walked in first again. He still had the long knife. Any hint of the humour he'd brought in with him on the previous visit had vanished. Their last encounter had clearly damaged his ego and it looked like he'd come to make good on that.

Sharon and Dan also walked in behind him like they had the last time they'd visited.

Each of Home's guards had tension in their form, defensive as if they expected Flynn to be a prick to them again. Understandably so. But the long hours in the dark had given him a chance to reassess. Whatever beef he had with them couldn't get in the way of the people in Home's safety. The Queen would attack at some point. She would kill the pregnant woman in the watery cell along with all of the others in there. Maybe some of them were pregnant too. The longer he spent behaving like a twat, the less chance he'd have of preventing it.

Not an apology, but Flynn opened his mouth to break the ice. However, before he could say anything, the guards parted and Rose walked in behind them. He let out the slightest gasp at the sight of her.

Like Flynn, Rose had been given new clothes. She even looked like she'd washed, her long blonde hair shimmering in the daylight behind her. She beamed a warm smile at him, which he returned.

It took a second for Flynn to see she had a tray in her hands. It had a cup and a bowl on it. The smell of stew wafted towards him.

Once Rose had placed the tray on the bed, Flynn reached out and squeezed her hand. He then picked up the cup of water, his throat so dry it felt like it had cracked.

"Not too quick," Rose said. "You don't want to be sick."

The cup pressed to his dry lips and a desire to knock the entire thing back, Flynn took just one small sip and put it back down on the tray. She had a point. They'd not given him much to drink in what could have been days in that room, he didn't want to fill his stomach immediately.

"Once you've eaten that," Brian said and pointed down at Flynn's stew with his long knife, "you can address the people of Home like you want to."

Flynn nodded. Hard to accept Brian had any control over him, but he did. The sooner he put his ego to one side, the easier it would be to move forward.

"No funny business though." This time Brian pointed the knife straight at Flynn and it took all Flynn had to let him. "I'll be standing behind you. If I get even a whiff of nonsense, I'll cut your fucking throat."

Again, Flynn swallowed down his reaction, his snarky

response running to the edge of his tongue and stopping there. He had to think of the people in Home and the women in the water. They deserved to live more than he deserved to serve his pride. Let Brian threaten him; he could rise above it.

The smell of the broth made Flynn's stomach rumble. A nod at Brian, Sharon, and Dan, and he opened his mouth. He might have tasted the stew a thousand times before, but that didn't stop the warm familiarity of it lighting him up.

CHAPTER 36

It hadn't been long since he'd walked down the corridors of Home as a resident, but in that time, Flynn had seen so much it felt like a lifetime ago. The lack of change in the place unsettled him. The sun still shone down through the grates. The place still smelled of earth and dust. The linoleum floor still had scratches and gashes in it. He felt like no more than a guest now. The sooner they dealt with the Queen and her bullshit, the better. It was definitely time for him to move on.

Flynn marched down the corridor with Rose beside him. Brian and his unreasonably long knife walked behind them. Dan and Sharon walked in front.

"I've missed you," Flynn said to Rose and reached across to hold her warm hand. To his relief, she reciprocated. The time in the dark had given him space to think. He'd missed many opportunities with her. Their number could be up at any point in this brutal world, he couldn't die knowing he didn't make a move. Too scared to take action in case his fragile ego took a beating. He needed to grow the fuck up and be an adult about it.

The sound of footsteps ahead pulled Flynn's attention up the corridor. When he saw Angelica, butterflies shimmered through his stomach. Not that he missed her, but something about the intimacy he'd once shared with her made him feel vulnerable. Especially as he now walked with Rose's hand in his.

As much as the coward in Flynn wanted to let go of Rose's hand, he didn't. In fact, he squeezed it tighter. Fuck you, Angelica.

Dan and Sharon parted for Angelica, and although Flynn smiled at her and went to move aside, she stared straight at Rose, knocking shoulders with her on the way past.

"Hey!" Flynn said, but Angelica ignored him, sidestepping Brian and walking off down the corridor.

"I said *hey*!" Still nothing from Angelica. "You crazy bitch."

When Angelica spun around to face Flynn, he stopped and stared at her. "What's wrong with you, you nutter?"

Fire swirled through her eyes as she glared at him, but she didn't reply. Instead, she spun around and walked off again.

When Angelica had gone from his sight, Flynn looked at Rose and shrugged. "What the fuck was that about? Has anything gone on between you two?"

"She's been a bitch since I got here. Are you sure she finished it with you? She's behaving like it might have been the other way round."

Brian tutted behind them. "Come *on*! Sort your drama out in your own time."

A shake of his head and Flynn walked off again, still holding Rose's hand. "Yeah," he said, "she definitely ended it with me." He smiled at her. "And I'm so glad she did."

CHAPTER 37

They'd set the crowd up so Flynn had to stand in front of Serj's memorial grave to address them. Before he looked at all the people there, he looked down at the inscription on the headstone. They'd done it since he'd left. It read:

Leader, mentor, friend.

A LUMP LIFTED IN FLYNN'S THROAT AND HE DREW A DEEP breath to combat it. It helped when Rose grabbed his hand and gave it a squeeze. He had this. He could do it.

When Flynn looked up at the sea of familiar faces, he smiled. "It's nice to see you all."

Some of the people smiled back, the July sunshine illuminating their warmth. Some, like Larry and the guards, didn't. To see Maggie, one of the teenagers who'd gotten on really well with Serj, gave Flynn another lift. She beamed a grin at him. At least some people were pleased to see him.

"You've had years of relative peace in Home." Flynn's voice echoed over the silent crowd. "Some of the kids probably don't even remember Moira." A look at Sharon and Dan, he sighed. Their three would have been old enough now to get involved in this new fight.

"And believe me, not remembering that crazy bitch is a good thing. Some of you probably don't remember Vicky either." Tension snapped through the three guards, and when Flynn looked at Brian, he saw his knife twitch in his grip. "She was a great woman who knew how to deal with Moira, and all of you can thank her for your lives in Home now."

"And for the virus," Brian muttered so only Flynn and Rose heard him.

"But I'm afraid you have another threat coming your way. She's called the Queen and she's fucking insane."

Rose stood slightly behind Flynn, so he grabbed her hand and pulled her next to him. "This is Rose. She and I met when we were imprisoned by the Queen. The Queen finds people by catching them out in the wild, or by promising travellers a better life than the one they currently have. She claims to give them food, shelter, and protection—the three things most people need in this world. But then she makes them compete in several brutal games that see all of them die until there's only one person left. At least, that's how she frames it to her community. There are limited spaces in the royal complex, so they can only help one. Might as well make a sport of it, eh?"

Twists of disgust shaped some of the staring faces.

"Well, we've since found out that the Queen and those closest to her eat the bodies of the people who die in the games. Turns out, the games are much more about feeding that greedy bitch than they are about offering one person salvation."

Wherever Flynn looked in the crowd, he now saw a

frowning face staring back at him. Even Maggie. And why wouldn't they? Who wanted to hear about someone like the Queen? Especially when she would be coming for them in the near future.

"I've seen what she does when she comes into a community. Rose has seen what she does. She kills *everyone* and steals their resources."

Not aggressive, but one of the crowd spoke up. "How do you know she'll attack us?"

"She's said she will," Flynn said. "Several times. I mean, the choice is yours; you can risk that she won't and hope everything works out, or you can be ready for it. With preparation, she won't stand a chance."

"People say a lot of things," the man in the crowd said, the wind tossing his short hair. "Don't make it true."

A shrug and Flynn nodded. "They do. You can *say* you don't want my help and I can walk away. If I'm being honest, I'd rather you said that. It means I don't have to risk my life for a community I have no desire to stay in. But I had to come back here and warn you. What you do with this information is your choice."

Before the man could say anything else, a woman stepped forward. Flynn recognised her from when she'd arrived at Home fairly recently. Her name was Ellie and she'd turned up about as pregnant as the woman in the water pit. She now had a small child in her arms. "I know the woman he's talking about. I was in her community. She's crazy and doesn't allow anyone to have children because she can't have them herself. Whenever a woman in her community got pregnant, they disappeared. But people kept having sex"—she flushed red—"because that's what we do, right? The only problem being that the withdrawal method isn't very reliable."

Flynn looked at Rose and saw her eyes were glazed. She must have been thinking about the Queen's fuck toy too.

Ellie reached out to her partner, Aaron. "We got pregnant and knew we couldn't stay. Everyone lived in fear of her. So we got out and found Home."

Brian stepped forward and threw his arms up. "And why are we only finding out about this now?"

Flynn looked from the bearded man to the woman and back to him again. "It's not her fault, Brian."

Before Brian could respond, Ellie said, "We didn't know the people here. What if someone spoke to her regularly? We didn't want her finding us, and we didn't want to be associated with her and her actions. Everything Flynn's said is true. She's insane, and if she sets her sights on Home, you'd best be ready for her."

Where Flynn thought he had silence from the crowd before, it now dropped to a whole new level. Instead of focusing on him, the gathered crowd now looked at one another. They needed to make a decision for their safety.

After a few seconds, the crowd broke into a hushed chat and Flynn spoke to Brian, Sharon, and Dan in a loud enough voice for everyone to hear him. "Now you've heard about the Queen, you need to decide if you want my and Rose's help. Alternatively, you can wait here like sitting ducks and we'll be on our merry way."

Flynn grabbed Rose's hand and led her away from Serj's memorial stone. "We'll be in the canteen. Come and find us when you've made your minds up."

As they walked, Flynn spoke so only Rose could hear him. "You were thinking about that man she killed in the plaza too, eh?"

A deep sigh as she held her head up and stared at Home's entrance, Rose said, "Yep."

CHAPTER 38

❦

Flynn sat opposite Rose at one of the canteen's old tables. He watched her look around the place, her mouth open as she took everything in. "It looks a lot different than it used to," he said.

Still looking around, Rose said, "I can imagine. I'm trying to picture it."

To think of the old days made Flynn smile. "We'd all gather here. With the diseased outside, it seemed like the perfect place to hang out. I'd sit with Vicky, Serj, and the other guards most of the time. Although sometimes I'd ignore her. I was *horrible* to her when I was a teenager."

"You're supposed to be horrible as a teenager."

Despite the sadness of how he'd treated Vicky, Flynn smiled. "Serj said that too. I just wish we'd been on better terms. Had I known I wouldn't see her again, I would have made much better use of our time together. At that age, it felt like everyone was going to be around forever. Especially Vicky. We'd survived the worst of it and come out the other side." The sting of tears itched his eyes and he blinked repeatedly. "I'm sorry." He fanned his face. "It's just being back here …"

Rose reached across the table and held both of his hands in hers. "It's okay. It's important you feel it. This world has thrown a lot of shit at us. If we don't allow ourselves to be honest and let the pain in, it'll eat us alive."

A deep inhale pulled in the dusty reek of the canteen. Flynn also smelled the tang of cabbage. Maybe in his memory, maybe such a part of the room it still smelled of it. He continued to look around the place. "We had electricity for the longest time. The field behind the front door used to have solar panels in it."

"The one with all the tubes in it now?"

A raised eyebrow and Flynn put on a mock serious voice, his vision still blurred from where his tears hadn't completely cleared. "Our water management system, don't you mean?"

Rose laughed. "Terribly sorry, old chap. Do beg your pardon."

Still swamped with sadness, Flynn tried to smile through it. "We used to have screens running all the time so we could see if there were any threats outside. It all seemed a bit gross after half the community fell to the diseased. I couldn't look at them for a while for fear of seeing a familiar face. Little did I know that Vicky was one of them. Probably a good thing I didn't find that out then. I don't know what I would have done. At sixteen, I could fight, but I doubt I would have survived on my own out there. God knows I would have tried though."

When Rose squeezed Flynn's hands, he snapped away from his spiralling thoughts and looked into her deep brown eyes. "I'm glad I met you, Rose. You've made everything a *lot* easier. My will to keep going was starting to ebb."

"And then you met me in a dark, dank dungeon where

you were about to be branded like cattle. It's all anyone would need for an epiphany, right?"

The first genuine laugh since Flynn had been in the canteen, the sound of it echoed through the empty space. "Even with all of that, I knew you were special. If nothing else, you intrigued me enough to make me want to find out more." He blushed as he said it and stared down at their clasped hands. "Kinda helps that you're smoking hot too."

When Flynn looked up, he found Rose staring at him. Because he'd already wasted opportunities, he couldn't waste this one. He half stood up and leaned across the table towards her.

Time stood still, and for a moment he didn't think she'd meet him in the middle. But then she got to her feet and moved towards him, her lips slightly puckered.

A loud bang suddenly went off inside one of the two corridors leading deeper into Home. It happened in the corridor farther away from them, and at the other end from where they were.

They stopped—both still leaning over the table with just a few inches between their faces—and stared in the direction of it, waiting for something to happen.

"What the fuck was that?" Rose said.

Before Flynn could reply, a banshee wail rang through the empty complex. So loud, her scream sounded like it came from several places at once. After he'd stared at the corridor for another second and not seen her come out, he looked back at Rose. "Does that answer it for you? I'm guessing Angelica was watching us about to kiss."

A shake of her head and Rose's eyes spread wide as she sat back down again. "If you mean that much to her, why did she split up with you?"

The moment of romance had gone thanks to his crazy ex.

Flynn shrugged and sat down too. "Fuck knows. She obviously liked playing me and Larry off one another. Now she's lost control of that, she's showing her true colours. She's fucking mental."

"Pure control freak," Rose said.

The march of footsteps took their attention away from Angelica. They entered the room before the people did. They came from the direction of Home's foyer. Both Flynn and Rose watched the space they would enter through.

Brian, Sharon, and Dan appeared, walked over to the table, and remained on their feet when they got there. Where Flynn had expected Brian to speak, it caught him off guard when Dan did. "We want to stop her."

"I think that's a good idea."

Sharon spoke this time. "So what do we do?"

"Well, seeing as I've had a bit of time to think …" Flynn lowered his voice to admonish the guards, "being locked in a dark cell and all …"

None of them replied, so he continued. "I reckon the best time to surprise them will be during one of their twisted games. There's so much going on, it'll be easy enough for us to hide in the town while everyone's distracted. We can then come out of the buildings when there's a big crowd. If we co-ordinate our attacks, we can take down the royal complex's muscle before they know what's hit them."

This time Brian spoke. "And what about the rest of them? They're a large community, right?"

"I reckon we can persuade them not to fight," Flynn said. "Once we cut the head off the snake, they'll see they're free. As much as they bow down to the Queen, I can't see them caring when she's gone. Especially if half of them want a life she won't let them have."

Silence swept through the place before Dan looked at Rose and said, "And what do you think?"

Rose flushed red. It clearly caught her off guard to be asked by Flynn's previous community. After a moment's silence, Flynn saw her visibly relax and she said, "I can't think of a better option than what's been put forward."

"So when's the next games?" Sharon asked.

After he'd looked at Rose and she offered him nothing, Flynn turned to the guards. "I'd say soon from what we saw, but I don't know. Rose and I can go to the town and scope it out." Another look at Rose. "That okay with you?"

She shrugged and nodded yes.

"And how do we know you'll come back?" Brian said.

"You know I didn't have to come here in the first place, right? If I didn't care about the people in Home, I'd be a million miles from here by now."

The hard frown on Brian's face suggested he wanted to argue with Flynn, but he had nothing. Instead he shrugged and said, "Fine, I'm trusting you on this."

"You don't have a choice, Brian."

A shake of his head and Brian walked away from them. When he'd left the canteen, Dan looked at Flynn. "Go easy on him, yeah? You've taken your pound of flesh with the whole pissing-himself thing. Nothing can bring Vicky back, just like nothing can bring our kids back. We appreciate what you're doing for us, and I think it's time we moved on."

It went against every instinct in him, but Flynn let go of his anger and nodded at Dan. "Can someone get us some food and drink before we leave?"

Dan nodded, his eyes smiling, even though the rest of him didn't. "Of course."

CHAPTER 39

Flynn and Rose had kept up a quick pace on their return to the Queen's town. Rose entered the hotel foyer first and Flynn followed her in. The large space made him feel exposed and he looked everywhere he could think of. Too many places for people to hide in. As always happened, Rose moved as if on a carpet of air and his clumsy steps called out their presence to anyone who wanted to listen.

Rose ran through the doorway to the ground floor first and Flynn followed behind. The stale brown and red carpet at least muted his steps, even if it did stink of rot.

It made sense to return to the same spot they'd been in before, so Flynn followed Rose when she turned down the corridor with the window at the end of it.

Like before, they stood far enough back so they wouldn't be seen, but close enough to the window to be able to view the plaza. Both of them breathed heavily from their quick pace. The Queen had mentioned twelve prisoners a few days back. How close was she to twenty?

Because Flynn wanted to get as close to the window as possible, he pressed against Rose and looked out. He loved the way she smelled. Even in a world with no perfume and irregular showers, her natural odour gave her skin a flat and calming smell. Not like Angelica, who had a strong acidic reek to her. Almost as if the poison inside her oozed from her pores.

To look at the watery prison out in the plaza spiked Flynn's pulse and his stomach turned over against itself. How did the women cope in there? Why weren't there any men in with them?

As hard as Flynn looked, he couldn't see her. His stomach sank. They'd left it too long. He should have done more out in the meadows and made sure her and her partner didn't run into the Queen.

But then, in one corner, holding onto the bars above her head, he saw the brown hair of the pregnant woman. Not quite relief because she had to exist in that watery hell, but at least they still had a chance of getting her out.

When Rose leaned back into Flynn, he took the press of her body. She didn't ask him to step back, so he put an arm around her waist and continued to look outside. A lazy atmosphere hung over the plaza. Hours must have passed out there where nothing happened.

Not only had Home fed Flynn and Rose, but they'd given them weapons. Rose had gone for a sword and machete. Flynn had also taken a machete and had a crossbow strapped to his back. Now much more able to cope with any threats, he felt slightly more confident than he had the last time they'd been in the town.

Just one guard stood out in the plaza. A hunter, he had a dark scowl and stubble on his square jaw. He stood over the pit with the women in it. The women barely moved and he looked beyond bored, his eyes half closed as he rocked like he could fall asleep at any moment. No doubt the Queen always had someone on guard, standing there for hours on end, doing nothing but waiting. No way would she risk letting the women escape. If it got back to the royal complex what she did to them, maybe she'd lose her tenuous grip on the power she had over the place. Flynn and Rose would get the women out of there so they could take the truth back to the royal complex with them.

Since Home had dressed Flynn in a sweatshirt when he'd been unconscious, he now sweated harder than he would have in his T-shirt. In any other situation he would have moved away from the person's body heat next to him, but with Rose, he didn't care. He'd wait there forever and deal with the discomfort.

When Rose reached down to Flynn's hand on her stomach and stroked the back of it, Flynn's heart kicked and his breath caught in his throat. She then slowly turned around.

The pair stared at one another for a second, Flynn getting lost in Rose's dark eyes. Their lives were at risk in this town. They might not make it out. Maybe destined to die, maybe not, he couldn't wait any longer.

Flynn leaned down to kiss Rose and she stood on her tiptoes to meet him. She pressed her full lips against his and a buzz ran through him, so strong he could almost hear it.

As they kissed, Flynn pulled Rose in tight, forceful with the passion he'd kept contained for so long. Rose twisted into his embrace.

They parted for a second and stared at one another, breathless with the intensity of their kiss. A slight glaze had spread across Rose's eyes as if intoxicated by it. Flynn felt the same. "Wow," he said. "You can't believe how long I've wanted to do that for."

Rose nodded. "Me too, even though it's probably not the most appropriate place for it."

Before Flynn could reply, the voice of a guard called through the hotel. It came from the same floor they were on. From the same corridor. Footsteps joined the sound. It suggested there were more than one. It suggested they were close.

The moment shattered, Flynn stared at Rose. She stared back, her eyes wide, her jaw limp. She let the air out of her lungs as she said, "Fuck!"

CHAPTER 40

◈

"What are we going to do?" Flynn whispered, breathless in his panic. Instead of looking at Rose, he watched the end of the corridor in the direction of the sound. He freed his crossbow from the harness across his back, pressed the stock into his shoulder, and looked down the barrel, waiting for something to aim at. Even if he only took one of them down before they were overwhelmed, it had to be better than none.

Rose moved close to him and whispered into his ear, "I want you to wait here and don't follow me."

He pulled his focus away from the end of the corridor and looked at her. "What are you going to do?"

"I have a plan. And it's important that you let me do it. We need to serve the greater good, don't *ever* forget that. At present, you're more important than me. You can go back to Home and get an army ready. They won't listen to me."

"But we can get out of this together."

"Can you hear how many there are?"

The march of steps sounded like at least six to eight guards headed towards them. Flynn didn't reply.

"We won't last two seconds against them. At least this way, you can help everyone."

"But—"

"Let me do this, Flynn. I trust you'll find a way to help me, but it's not now, okay?"

Flynn lowered his crossbow as he fought against the sadness twisting through him. Not entirely sure what she had planned, but certain he wouldn't like it. "I can't lose anyone else."

"Make sure you come back, then." Before Flynn could reply, she said, "Besides, *I* can swim."

"What if the Queen tries to kill you straight away?"

"It's not her style. She likes ceremony too much. Besides, she'll want you too. Maybe she'll see me as bait."

Cold dread sank through Flynn, but he stayed put while she walked away from him towards the sounds at the end of the corridor. There seemed to be a logic in what she'd said and he certainly had nothing better to offer. He'd have to find a way to rescue her and liberate the people of the royal complex. But he'd do it. Especially if her life depended on it.

As Rose walked up the corridor, she dropped her machete and sword. Best to appear as non-threatening as possible.

The urge to follow her still pulled on Flynn, but then he listened to the people approaching. Too many for them both to take down, and they'd both be spotted if one of them didn't do something. What if they were both spotted anyway?

Too late to do anything about it, Flynn watched Rose step out into the next corridor. She'd sprung the plan on him, and although she'd convinced him, it already seemed like an awful idea. What if she'd gotten it wrong and they killed her straight away? But what could he do about it now?

A male voice shouted, "What the fuck are you doing here?"

"I'm sorry," Rose said, a forced vulnerability in her tone. "I've been hiding here for days now. I can't cope anymore. I'm tired and hungry. I want to go back to the royal complex."

Several men laughed at her. "You're hoping, aren't you?"

"Huh?"

"You've fucked the Queen over, love. You don't get to just come back into the royal complex. Now, on your knees, and hands behind your head."

Although he couldn't see her, Flynn listened to Rose drop to the ground. Torn between acting and remaining put, his crossbow shook as he raised it to his shoulder again and watched the end of the corridor. Rose had a point when she'd said Home would follow him. Besides, he could wait and see what they did to her. He could decide if he needed to come out fighting now, or if he'd have time to go back to Home. Either way, he couldn't simply leave Rose until he knew she'd be okay.

As the sound of footsteps marched away from Flynn, his heart sank. But he fought against it. Whatever happened, he wouldn't lose another person.

CHAPTER 41

A few minutes had passed since the sounds of the guards had vanished down the hallway, marched through the hotel's foyer, and gone outside. Flynn stared out of the small window at the plaza beyond.

When the stomp of what sounded like several guards entered the square, he watched the hunter by the pit look in the direction of the noise.

"Where did you find *her*?" the hunter asked.

"In that hotel. Says she's been in there for days. Where's the Queen?"

"Here." Her sharp call sounded like the caw of a crow as she emerged from an alleyway on the other side of the plaza, her angular face twisted as if she had a bad taste in her mouth. "Well, I never thought I'd see *you* again. And where's lover boy?"

"Gone," Rose said, still acting weak. "Once we'd escaped, he went back to Home and his girlfriend."

Flynn shook his head. They hadn't agreed on that. Rose had made him think she'd let the Queen know he'd be coming for her. It would make her worth keeping alive.

A tilt of her head and the Queen pushed her bottom lip out in mock sympathy. "Aw, poor you. Dumped by your boyfriend before you're even an item. And after all you did for him."

"Fuck you," Rose said.

The Queen laughed for a second and then her mirth fell. She spoke in monotone. "Put her in the pit."

Flynn shouldn't have agreed to her plan. Nausea turned over in his stomach to see the hunter by the pit snap the bolt open and rip the cage up. The hands holding onto it let go and the women already in there gasped as they trod water. Some held onto the edges, the brown-haired pregnant woman being one of them.

Before they could shove her, Flynn watched Rose jump into the water. Better to take what control she had.

The slam of the gate crashed through the plaza and echoed off the walls of the buildings surrounding it before the hunter cracked the bolt back into place.

Flynn watched the Queen down the barrel of his crossbow. One bolt through the window into her head and she'd be done for. But one bolt wouldn't take down an army. They needed to attack when they had enough people to go to war. At present, Rose's life wasn't in immediate danger.

After the Queen had walked onto the bars over the pit, stamping on the hands that tried to hold on, she smiled. "The good news for you lot is we won't be eating you any time soon. You'll all get to swim in there for another week at least. It'll soften you up if nothing else, make you a little more tender. I should probably throw some seasoning in with you." She laughed at her own joke and some of the hunters smiled with her.

"We have twenty prisoners in the dungeon. That means

we'll have the games tomorrow and enough meat to last us for a good few days."

Flynn lowered his crossbow. Rose could last the night in that pit if he left her there. The guard in the plaza would make it too hard to bust her out just on his own. He stepped away from the window. If he could get back to Home and bring an army, they could free Rose and the others. She'd be okay for one night.

By the time he'd reached the end of the corridor, Flynn couldn't hear the Queen's words anymore, but her vicious cackle called through the town, turning his blood cold.

Just one more day and he'd get the chance to cave her fucking head in. Flynn turned his back on the corridor, the Queen, and Rose, and took off towards the hotel's foyer at a jog. Hopefully all the guards were in the plaza so he could get out of there without incident.

CHAPTER 42

The uneven ground sent Flynn's feet twisting and turning as he walked over it. He'd been on the move for hours, the thought of Rose in the watery pit driving him on. That and the Queen's plan to have another set of games tomorrow. They didn't have any time to fuck around.

When Flynn left the Queen's town, it had been late evening. The air had gradually cooled as it welcomed the chill of night. He'd not seen anyone on his walk, but that didn't stop him keeping a hold of his crossbow with both hands as he moved through the long grass. Before he'd left the town, he'd decided he'd shoot first and ask questions later. Nothing could get in the way of him saving Rose. Nothing.

It stood as a silhouette on the horizon for the longest time, but when Flynn got close to Home's gates, he saw Brian standing guard on one of the watchtowers. The man stared down at him. Hard to tell in the poor light, but it looked like the bearded arsehole thought about not opening up.

However, when Flynn got to within a few steps of the

front gates, Brian whistled down into the complex. The gates wobbled before they opened a crack for him.

"Thought you might have gotten yourself killed," Brian said from his elevated perch.

"You sound disappointed," Flynn said as he continued walking. Fuck Brian and his stupid little mind games.

∽

IT DIDN'T TAKE LONG FOR FLYNN TO ROUND EVERYONE UP. The entire community gathered in Home's dusty canteen. To look at them reminded him of the days of the diseased when every meeting had been conducted in the space. He looked at the dusty monitors, the paint peeling off the walls, and several broken tables piled in the corner. The thought of Vicky, Serj, and Piotr threatened to overwhelm him, but he pushed it down.

The room watched Flynn as he paced up and down in front of them. A look at all the familiar faces, he paused on Angelica's twisted expression before moving on. "The Queen's having one of her games tomorrow." His voice echoed through the near silent room.

"Where's your girlfriend?" Angelica asked.

Flynn looked at Larry next to her. The concern his new girlfriend had about Rose's whereabouts clearly made him uncomfortable. "You mean Rose?"

"Whatever," Angelica said.

"She's been captured."

Not enough of a smile to be overt about it, Angelica's eyes glowed at the news.

Flynn didn't realise he'd balled his fists until he saw Angelica looking down at them. Her pleasure gave way to fear. After letting his hands fall loose again, he shook his head at the jealous cow. It wouldn't get him anywhere to fall out with her. Instead, he put his attention on the gathered crowd. "I need as many people as possible to come with me. The Queen's coming for Home and we have a chance to stop her tomorrow. If we wait for her to come here, she'll roll right over you. Tomorrow, we can catch her with her pants down."

"And we'll help you rescue lover-girl," Angelica said.

Most of the room ignored Angelica. Instead they looked at Flynn with stoic and pale faces.

"I have a plan that will work," Flynn said. "It doesn't come without its risks, but it will stop the Queen before she can come here. I need you to trust me like you trusted Vicky all those years ago. This is for Home, not me. Once this is all done, Rose and I plan to walk away and leave this area forever—"

"I thought you said she's been captured?" Angelica said. "She can't exactly walk away if she's being held hostage."

Flynn ignored her again. "So, to reiterate, I'm doing this for your benefit, not mine. The more people who come and fight with me, the more likely it is you'll be able to spend another decade safe within these walls."

"Hang on." Angelica stepped forward and the room focused on her. "How do we know we can trust you? You say it's not, but how do we know this isn't just a rescue mission to help your little girlfriend?"

Many of the faces in the canteen turned on Flynn, awaiting an answer.

"I mean," Angelica continued, "it's rather convenient that now she's in need of help, the games are also happening tomorrow. It might just be me, but it seems rather serendipitous."

To think of the decisions he'd made regarding Rose, and now to have Angelica question it, flipped Flynn's switch. He marched over to Angelica and leaned into her face. Jaw clenched, he spoke through gritted teeth. "I *left* her there rather than save her so I could come back here. If it was all about Rose, I would have waited until the one guard over the watery pit she's currently in was on his own, killed him, and then run a fucking mile. Instead, I'm risking her *life* to come back here to help this community. To leave her there means the Queen doesn't know I'm on to her. It means we can take her down before she takes you down. Believe me, if it was just you, I would have gone for option A and saved a woman far greater than you'll ever be. As it is, there are a lot of people here worth saving. A lot of people I care about."

Angelica's face reddened.

A look at Larry, his frame coiled tight as if he might attack him, and Flynn shook his head. "And look at what you're doing to *him*. He's falling for you. If he's lucky, you'll land in someone else's bed soon and he'll see the fortunate escape he's had."

Although Angelica opened and closed her mouth, she clearly had nothing to say. Flynn watched her squirm. He looked at the rest of the canteen and they all watched on.

As the tension wound tighter in the room, Flynn refused to say anything, prolonging Angelica's discomfort.

A few seconds later, Angelica screwed her face up, shook her head, and ran out of the room, leaving Larry all on his own.

Maggie—the teenager Serj had gotten on with so well—broke the silence when she stood up and said, "I'm with you, Flynn."

Dan and Sharon got to their feet. "It goes without saying," Dan said. "We may have argued in the past, but I trust your plans. If even just a fraction of Vicky has rubbed off on you, you're the best person to lead this battle."

Flynn stared at Dan for a few seconds, the mention of Vicky clearly upsetting Dan as much as it did him. Not an apology, but an acknowledgement of what he'd done.

Over the next thirty seconds or so, many more of Home's residents stood up in answer to Flynn's call. Maybe fifty in total, they'd be a match for the Queen's hunters and guards even if they didn't have surprise on their side.

When everyone had finished standing up, Flynn nodded at the group. "Thank you for trusting me. I promise you, your well-being is at the forefront of my mind. We'll get through this with as few casualties as possible. However, I can't guarantee anyone's safety."

Silence met Flynn's words. Many of the people there hadn't ever fought before. Too young ten years ago, they were now the strength in Home.

"Now get your weapons and supplies," Flynn said, "and meet me back here in thirty minutes. We have to move into the city while it's dark. That way, we'll be set up and ready to take the Queen and her guards down when they all gather for the games tomorrow."

CHAPTER 43

Another walk of about three hours and Flynn finally led the fifty or so people from Home into the Queen's town. The moon hung full in the sky and provided a spotlight for them to navigate by. Despite another change of clothes, he ended up soaked again from the long dewy grass, but at least they'd made it. One more night of discomfort to take the bitch down would be more than worth it. After that he'd have to find somewhere to stay on a more permanent basis. The amount of travelling he'd had to do over the past few days had gone beyond tedious.

Anxiety gnawed away at Flynn as he led the mob through the derelict scattering of offices and previously commercial buildings. Everywhere seemed abandoned and they kept to the shadows, but with every building housing an inky void, the Queen's people could be watching them from any one of thousands of windows. But they had the right intention. They were here to do the right thing. Hopefully luck would be on their side. Also, in such a large town, it would be unfortunate for them to be seen on the one of hundreds of paths they could have taken. Other than the plaza, he'd not witnessed evidence that the Queen put any stock in security. She'd probably have a skeleton crew watching the prisoners and not much else. Especially as the rest of her community would be preparing for the games in the morning.

It didn't take long to get to their destination. Flynn didn't know which building he would use, but when he saw a large abandoned office block in the perfect location, it seemed like as good an option as any. It also got them off the streets.

Grit covered the floor inside the office space, the crunch of their footsteps calling out to anyone close enough to hear them. Not that they needed to worry about that; if they were close enough to hear them, they would have already seen them by now.

Flynn led the group to a large window looking out over the square with the police station in it. He pointed at the building, the *P* and *O* of 'Police' having fallen from the sign. "When Rose and I did the games," he said in a whisper to the huddled crowd, "we were brought to this building. We were given a night's sleep in there, but from what the Queen said, they're doing the games in one day this time. She said she wants to get to Home as soon as possible. We may have to wait for a few hours, but all of the people from the royal complex will gather here at some point today. Because I don't know where the first of the trials are held, this seems like the best place to wait. We know they'll come through here at some point."

A look up at the taut rope stretched from the police station's roof to the office block on the other side and he continued. "That's what they expect the prisoners to cross." The rings hung at regular intervals, swinging in the gentle breeze.

After most of the people had looked up at them, Flynn said, "Once they're all gathered here, I'm going to jump the Queen and kill her. I want to do that before the first person is made to swing from the rings. But whatever happens, you all need to follow my lead. Don't do *anything* until I've attacked the Queen. Something might change in the moment and I might have to go for a different approach. Once I've attacked her, that's your signal to lynch the royal guards and the hunters."

"How will we know who to attack?" Maggie said.

"Good question." Flynn took in all the wide eyes staring at him, hanging on his every word. "The royal guards all wear a dark blue uniform. They'll all have weapons. The hunters are the only other ones with weapons. If they're not armed, leave them alone."

The faces continued to stare at him, but no one else spoke.

"Before they swing across the rings," Flynn said, "they'll climb up shit slope."

"Shit slope?" Larry said.

To look at Angelica's lover ran a deep unease through Flynn. He hadn't wanted him to come. Not because he gave a fuck about Angelica, more because he wanted to make sure he could trust everyone to have his back. But Brian, Sharon, and Dan had insisted on bringing Larry. The best shot in Home by a mile, they needed his skills. Flynn said, "It's a tall slope made slick with sewage and it has spikes at the bottom."

Larry's jaw fell.

"They expect the prisoners to climb it. Those who slip end up impaled on the spikes."

Susan—a blonde lady in her thirties—said, "Then why don't we find the slope and jump them there?"

"Rose and I didn't see the Queen the last time we were

there. I don't think she turns up until they get to the police station. Besides, I wouldn't want to risk traipsing through the town to try to find it. We're better here."

Susan nodded.

"The square will fill with people before the prisoners are dragged up to the police station's roof," Flynn said. "We need to make sure we're hiding in the surrounding buildings. Distribute yourselves as evenly as possible, so when we come out and jump them, we're coming from every angle. We want to take them down before they know what's hit them."

∽

IT TOOK ABOUT TWENTY MINUTES TO GET EVERYONE IN PLACE after they'd divided into four groups. Dan went with one group, Sharon with another, Brian with the third, and Flynn took the last. They spread out and hid in the buildings surrounding the square. When the crowd gathered, the guards would be nullified in minutes.

Flynn felt weary from the past few days. Aches sat in his tired limbs and his heart hurt for Rose. So exhausted, he worried the lump in his throat would burst in front of everyone and he wouldn't be able to control it.

Just two people remained close to Flynn, a couple of boys called Jack and Ross. They were kids the last time Home went to war. They were barely men now. The others in his group scattered throughout the rooms on either side of them.

Jack and Ross lay slumped in the dark shadows as if asleep. And why wouldn't they be? They were probably exhausted like him and had no idea what they would be facing in the morning. Their ignorance would give them a few hours of peace.

If only Flynn could switch off like they had. Tired everything, he stood by the window looking out over the square and watched the space. At some point they'd see people file into it. At some point, he'd have to lead Home into battle like Vicky had done in the past. If he did half the job she had, most of them would walk away from this.

CHAPTER 44

It wouldn't do any harm to look. Ross and Jack were now definitely asleep. Their deep breathing called through the space, confirming what Flynn's eyes couldn't in the darkness. They wouldn't miss him.

A look out through the window again and he saw how the first signs of morning penetrated the night's sky. If he wanted to go, he had to do it now before it got too bright.

Out in the darkened corridors of the abandoned office block, Flynn's eyes stung from straining to see. The rooms closest to him were filled with the people from Home, so he ran on tiptoes to get past them unnoticed. He might have only been going to look, but if anyone saw him, it would understandably make them nervous about the risk he was taking. He'd be careful; besides, he needed to do it.

Despite all the walking Flynn had done over the past few days—aches deep in his bones every time he moved—he kept a quick pace. Not quite soundless as he walked, but he'd led a stampede of Home's residents to their hiding spots and gotten away with it. Surely one person moving through the night wouldn't cause too many problems.

To see the hotel he and Rose had gone through spiked a pang in his heart. Once he'd entered it, he would be close to her. How long would she last in that watery hell? At least she could swim; she wouldn't find it as unbearable as he would have.

Once inside, the large hotel foyer looked darker than he'd seen it before. The slight illumination of morning might have been affecting the night's sky, but it hadn't reached into the buildings yet.

Assaulted with the familiar smell of dust, Flynn ran across the dark amphitheatre of a room towards where he hoped the corridor to the first floor was. Hard to tell in such poor light.

Guided by his memory, Flynn found the doorway with relative ease. Despite his pulse running away with him, he tried to stay calm as he felt the softness of the grubby carpet beneath his steps.

As Flynn made muted progress towards his destination, he kept his stinging eyes spread wide. The shadowy corridor looked clear, but with rooms down either side, there could be guards in any one of them.

After he'd turned into the dead-end corridor, Flynn ran down it and stood a short distance away from the small window like he had with Rose. He could see the guard standing over the pit with the women in it, but the guard wouldn't be able to see him.

Hard to tell how many women remained in the pit in the plaza. The bright moon ran a highlight along the bars and their fingers, but it didn't show him who the fingers belonged to. He hoped one set of them belonged to Rose.

Just one guard stood between Flynn and the answers he needed. One guard keeping the women imprisoned. The rest were probably back at the royal complex with the Queen.

After he'd drawn a deep breath to still his nerves, Flynn pulled in a dry gulp and raised his crossbow. Now he'd come to look again, he knew he couldn't leave her.

The stock of the crossbow in his shoulder and pressed against his cheek, Flynn lined up the guard in his sights. Surely the others would be too busy with the games to notice the women had been busted out. Especially if they planned on doing everything in just one day.

Seeing the lie he told himself for what it was, Flynn tightened his squeeze on the trigger anyway and he drew a calming breath. He couldn't walk away from this again. Hopefully the pregnant woman remained in the pit too. He owed her.

Just before he could set the bolt free, the sound of footsteps ran down the corridor towards him.

"Fuck," Flynn whispered as he spun around, his crossbow still raised. He couldn't see much in the dark, but he didn't need to. The runner was closing in on him quickly.

CHAPTER 45

They might have thought they were running quietly down the hotel's corridor, but they weren't. Flynn had heard them from far enough away that he'd be ready for them. The second he saw them, they'd get a bolt in their face. Plenty of empty rooms in the hotel, it could take days before anyone found their dead body. By that time, he and the residents of Home would have made their presence known to the Queen.

Despite trying to find reassurance in his preparedness, Flynn's crossbow shook in his trembling grip. He'd been an idiot. Rose would have been all right if he'd left it. Now he ran the risk of jeopardising everything if the person from the royal complex managed to yell out before he killed them.

Two more steps and the silhouette of the person appeared. But before Flynn pulled the trigger, he saw they had their hands in the air. Their fingers were splayed, each one clearly visible as not having a weapon anywhere near it.

The person walked towards Flynn slowly. It looked like a man, his shoulders broader than any woman Flynn had seen —other than Mistress' maybe.

As much as Flynn felt a temptation to loose a bolt, his finger twitching on the trigger, they had their hands raised. They clearly didn't mean him any harm.

The man continued forward with slow and cautious steps. Flynn kept his crossbow raised. Surely they would have tried to attack him by now if they had anything to do with the Queen.

A deep inhale of the rot-infused air and Flynn watched the man step into a slash of moonlight. "Dan?"

At first, Dan didn't reply. Once he'd stepped close enough so he could keep his voice low, he pushed Flynn's crossbow down so it no longer pointed at him and sighed. "I know it's hard, mate."

"Like fuck! How would you know how this feels?"

"Okay." Dan shrugged. "I've not been in this exact situation, but I can imagine if that was Sharon out there, I'd struggle to leave her in that pit for any longer than I had to."

Dan passed Flynn and peered out through the window. When he turned around again, he wore a twist to his features at what he'd just seen. "You're right, I can't imagine how it must feel for you right now."

"It's night time. I could kill that guard, free Rose and all the women, and no one will find out until after the games. By then it will be too late." The same rationale Flynn had tried to trick himself with. To look at Dan showed he couldn't convince him either.

"You think no one will check on the women before the games?"

"Yeah." Even Flynn heard his own lack of conviction in his tone.

Dan didn't reply.

While pointing out of the window, Flynn whispered, "I'm

finding it hard to know she's right there and I'm doing *nothing* to help her."

"But you *are*."

"Huh?"

"You're planning on taking the Queen and her guards down. So not only are you doing something to help her, but you're doing something to help *everyone* affected by that bitch. What would Rose want you to do right now?"

While releasing a deep sigh, Flynn dropped his gaze. "There's a pregnant woman in there too. She must be at least eight months gone."

When Flynn looked back up, he saw the whites of Dan's eyes stand out in the darkness from where they'd widened.

"Rose and I saw her and her partner walking through a meadow. I had a chance to save them, but I chose not to put myself at risk. When they walked over the next hill, they bumped into the Queen and her mob. I didn't know they were there, but I knew the path they followed would lead to them eventually. The Queen killed her boyfriend and put her in the pit. I need to bust her out too."

"And you will, but you need to leave her for a few more hours. You need to use your head, Flynn."

"Like you used your head with Vicky, you mean? Is that what you're saying? I need to make a decision for the greater good, regardless of the consequences for the individuals."

After he'd drawn a deep breath, Dan spoke on the exhale. "There isn't a second that passes where I don't question that decision. It's been over ten years and the guilt of it still eats away at me. Second to my children dying, it's the greatest pain I have to live with. Sharon and I were angry and looking for someone to blame. We believed keeping Vicky in the community would be a risk to the stability of Home. I still believe that, in fact. At the time, we had one way of dealing with the people we needed to evict. It was the decision we made. I'm not sure we would make it again."

To see the tears in Dan's eyes took away some of Flynn's anger. It helped to know he regretted it, even though it wouldn't bring Vicky back.

"And I'm not asking you to sacrifice the lives of any of those prisoners," Dan said. "You said yourself they'll be too busy with the games tomorrow. Too busy to do anything to those women out there."

When Dan put an arm around Flynn's shoulders, Flynn tensed up at the touch. He'd wanted to kill the man not so long ago. But maybe he needed to move on. Nothing would bring Vicky back, and Dan had done the best he could in the moment. He'd followed protocol with her eviction. Maybe Vicky would have done the same if someone else had been responsible for letting loose the virus and killing most of the people she'd loved. And if he'd kept his fucking mouth shut, no one would have ever known about what she did in the first place.

The gentle tug from Dan encouraged Flynn to walk away. He resisted for a few seconds before yielding. Together they turned their backs on the window overlooking the plaza and the pit. He'd be back for Rose and the pregnant woman before they ran out of time.

CHAPTER 46

⁂

Flynn's anxiety rose and fell in waves as the morning wore on. They hadn't known the location of shit hill before, but they sure as hell heard it now. Screams and jeers came across the town to them. They seemed to last forever as Flynn relived his own horrific experience. Those poor bastards on the hill at that moment were no doubt scared, exhausted, and having to avoid a meteor shower of boulders from the crowd. But at least this would end today and the Queen would pay.

When the sounds finally died down, Flynn rolled some of his tension from his shoulders. He had several people from Home waiting with him, so he used hand gestures to tell them to hide. They'd agreed they wouldn't speak when the sun rose. They couldn't risk being overheard.

The people with him all moved out of the office they currently occupied and spread throughout the buildings overlooking their quarter of the square.

Flynn looked across the square through the window he stood by. When he saw Dan, he gave him a thumbs-up. He watched Dan turn away as if to check on the people with him.

He then looked back at Flynn and returned the affirmative gesture.

∽

About another fifteen minutes passed before the first of the crowd wandered into the square. Although several alleys and smaller roads led into the space, it had one main entrance and exit via what had once been a four-lane road.

The day had heated up and Flynn yawned as the sun shone through the glassless window next to him. He hadn't slept all night and his legs felt the effort of the past few days, but he'd find the surge of adrenaline to boost his energy when he needed it.

Careful to stay out of sight, Flynn watched as more and more people filled the large square, the taut rope stretched over it like a washing line. Fresh gusts of wind soared through the office building, eliciting moans and creaks from the huge structure. How long would it take for entropy to claim every building in the town?

Other than Dan on the opposite side of the square, Flynn couldn't see anyone else. The other people from Home had been given explicit instructions to hide until they got the signal. No doubt Sharon and Brian watched Dan, the leader for each section ready to tell their group to take action when the time came.

As more and more bodies filled the square, Flynn looked for the Queen. Or even her throne. Because everything hinged on taking her down, he'd picked the spot close to where she'd previously been. He'd try his crossbow first. If he could take her out from a distance, it would make everything a hell of a lot easier. Although deep down, he knew nothing would be easy over the next few hours.

Hunters came into the square, but Flynn hadn't seen a single royal guard yet. The occasional flash of blue fooled him momentarily, but it didn't belong to the Queen's personal protection. Just the coincidental clothes of a royal complex resident.

The creak of cartwheels cackled down the wide road and bounced off the buildings surrounding the square. Many of the people gathered there stopped to look in the direction of the noise. When Flynn saw the first of the caravan of barbaric trailers, he pulled in a sharp breath. The thick wooden stakes had claimed too many lives, the sharp poles stained with old blood.

Several hunters on each, they moved the carts into place in a line beneath the taut rope. There was still no sign of the Queen's throne.

Another look at Dan, Flynn saw him shrug. His gesture asked the same question Flynn had been thinking. *Where the fuck is she?*

Other than a shrug in return, Flynn had nothing. Fucked if he knew.

Like she'd been privy to their interaction, Flynn suddenly heard the Queen's sharp voice. The shrill and authoritative caw of a crow, it flew over the top of the spectators, but it came from an entirely different place than he'd expected. "Ladies and gentlemen ..."

Flynn lost track of the rest of her words as he turned to look at the police station's roof. From the distance between them, she should have looked small. But somehow, as she stood strong and straight, she looked like a giant. Like a god.

Just three prisoners stood in a line behind the Queen as she addressed the crowd. Why hadn't Flynn thought of it before. He'd forgotten about Mistress' pivotal role in the games until that moment. Of course someone would have to replace her. And it made sense for it to be the Queen.

A look back across at Dan in the abandoned shop opposite and Flynn pointed up at the police station. Not that he needed to point out the Queen to him.

Wide-eyed, Dan shrugged. *What do we do?*

Flynn pointed at himself and then pointed back at the Queen. He'd take her down.

A tilt of his head to one side, Dan looked to question Flynn's plan.

But Flynn nodded. He'd do it.

Although he stared at him, Dan didn't respond.

Flynn looked up at the Queen again, squinting because of the strong sun at her back, adding to her god-like appearance. She had a twist to her angular face that spoke of her clear enjoyment at the power she currently had. Three prisoners at her disposal and the crowd of people in the palm of her hand.

Flynn nodded to himself this time. He could do it. He had to do it. After freeing his crossbow from the harness on his back, he left the office he currently occupied and walked down the corridor of the old building in the direction of the police station. He could do it.

CHAPTER 47

Of all the people he'd seen in the square, Flynn hadn't yet seen a single royal guard. As he stood in the doorway of the old office and looked over the small road at the police station, he had to assume they were all in there.

Unlike the main road leading to the square, the one between Flynn and the police station stretched just one lane wide. He could dash across it in seconds.

Another look up at the roof showed him the Queen as she threw her arms in wild gestures with the theatrics of her speech. Not that he listened to a word of the bile that spewed from her toxic mouth.

Just three prisoners stood up there with her. If Flynn didn't hurry up, they'd all be on the rings before he reached them.

Reluctance pulled on Flynn's already heavy limbs and panic wound tight in his chest. His stomach turned over against itself and his breaths quickened. Another look up and down the skinny road and it seemed clear both ways. He'd only have to expose himself for the briefest moment.

Flynn pulled in a deep breath and made a run for it.

Rather than bursting through the doorway into the police station, he pulled up next to it and hid in the shadows. The door had once had a window in the centre of it. When he peered through the space, he saw the blue uniform of two guards right there in the foyer. They stood by what would have once been the help desk. Other than the two women, the rest of the area seemed clear. No doubt the others were deeper in the building.

Flynn had to get through the police station and the Queen's guards without alerting anyone outside. If the hunters twigged, they'd rush the place and he'd be fucked. The hunters and the guards were trained fighters. The people of Home needed surprise on their side to take them down.

The sound of the Queen's voice rang out like a fascist dictator. Flynn drew one final deep breath as he raised the stock of his crossbow to his shoulder. He closed one eye, looked down its barrel, and pushed the door open with his right foot.

The door creaked. The two guards looked over. Flynn pulled the trigger. The crossbow bucked. A bolt exploded from it. Blood burst from one of the guard's necks. She fell clutching her throat.

The slap of Flynn's feet echoed through the foyer. In three steps he reached the next guard. Machete ready, he brought it down on her head in a wide arc. The guard's skull gave way, and warm blood sprayed up Flynn's face.

As the guard fell, Flynn wrenched his machete free and turned to finish the other woman off, but she'd already died. Blood ran from both corpses, pooling on the floor. The guards had dropped their batons, but despite his urge to pick them up, he left them. They were of no use to him.

Out of breath already, Flynn ran on his tiptoes to the door separating him and the rest of the police station. No time to recover, he pressed his back against a nearby wall and wiped the blood from his face.

The small glassless window in the door sat no larger than a cigarette packet. It showed Flynn the corridor on the other side. The door must have been used for security back in the day. A card reader hung broken from the wall next to it.

When Flynn looked through the small window again, he saw just one guard on the other side. He pulled back, loaded his crossbow with another bolt, and then knocked on the door.

"Hello?" the guard said.

But Flynn didn't reply, he simply knocked again.

"Hello?"

The steps of the guard marched towards the door. Flynn watched the small window and listened to her getting close.

When a blue eye pressed up to the small hole, Flynn jabbed his machete into it. A quick jab, it went deep into her eye socket with a wet squelch. The gritty resistance of bone vibrated through the handle.

The woman fell back and Flynn quickly withdrew his knife before she could drag it down with her.

Because he had to push the door to get through, he had to use enough force to move the guard's body too. It took a bit of effort, but he managed to shove a wide enough gap to shimmy sideways through the small space.

Flynn grabbed her still-warm hands and dragged her clear. He might need to get out of there in a hurry.

Despite being blindfolded the last time he'd walked through the station, Flynn knew exactly where the door in front of him went. It accessed the roof. Just a flight of stairs now separated him and the Queen.

At the door, Flynn peered through the window hole.

However, before he could open it, he felt the press of a sharp tip into the soft spot at the base of his skull.

The voice of a woman issued a low growl. "Move, and I'll drive this knife straight into your brain, you fuck."

Flynn froze.

"Give me your weapons."

Unable to look at the woman for fear of cold steel turning his lights off, Flynn lowered his crossbow for her to take. As she pulled it away, she also ripped his machete free from his belt.

"Go and get help," the woman said and Flynn listened to a second guard run off towards the foyer.

"We're going to wait here until backup arrives," the royal guard said. "Then I'm going to take you up to the roof and see what the Queen wants to do with you."

A deep sigh and some of Flynn's strength left him. He'd fucked it up. No way would the people of Home be able to hijack the square now. By revealing himself, he'd just negated their advantage. No other options left, he could only hope they'd see that and save themselves by getting out of there.

Flynn pressed his forehead against the door in front of him and let go of a deep sigh. He'd just fucked up Rose's chances of escape too.

CHAPTER 48

Flynn kept his forehead pressed against the metal door between him and the stairs leading to the roof of the building. The cold touch of it paled compared to the sharp tip of the royal guard's knife at the base of his skull. Just enough pressure so she didn't puncture the skin, but if she pushed much harder, the frigid steel would sink into him.

"Did you really think it would be that easy?" the guard said.

There didn't seem any point in replying, so Flynn kept his mouth shut, pressing his lips together to make sure he kept the words in. They'd kill him sooner or later, better he kept some pride by holding his tongue.

A loud click then snapped to the left of Flynn. Too scared to move, he listened to the *whoosh* of a bolt flying at him. When the pressure of the knife against the back of his head pulled away, followed by the thud of a body hitting the ground, Flynn turned around to look first at the dead guard and then at the doorway leading to the foyer. "Dan?"

"I figured you'd need the help. Good job I followed you, eh?"

"How far did the other guard get?" Flynn said. "Did she make it out into the square? Do the hunters know what's happening?"

Dan shook his head. "No, we're still in the clear. She didn't make it any farther than the foyer." A look at the door in front of Flynn, he said, "Are we going up, then?"

Flynn rubbed the back of his head. It itched and nothing more. Adrenaline from the close call sent a shake through him, but it would pass. After he'd retrieved his crossbow and machete from the now dead guard, he nodded. "Yeah, let's do this."

The window in the door didn't reveal much of the other side to them, so Flynn slowly pulled it open, his crossbow loaded and ready to fire.

He walked through to find the space empty. The metal stairs in front of them invited them up, the smell of iron hanging in the air like blood.

When Flynn had moved closer to the stairs and peered up through the gap between them, he saw just one guard. She stood at the top and had her face pressed to a crack in the door leading to the roof. She obviously watched the Queen.

Still shaking from the adrenaline of his last encounter, Flynn took several breaths as he raised his crossbow and pointed it up the stairs. Just one chance to make the shot. If he fucked up, she'd let everyone know they were there. And they couldn't get any closer to her to make the shot easier. One foot on the stairs and the sound of the metal steps would give them away.

When Dan leaned close to Flynn and whispered, "You've made this kind of shot a thousand times before," it helped calm him down.

"Just pretend her head's a rabbit," Dan added.

Next to Larry, Flynn had been one of the best shots in

Home. And because they didn't have Larry with them at that moment, it made sense for him to shoot her.

His usual preparation, Flynn filled his lungs with a deep breath, slowly let it out again, and held it. A squeeze of the trigger and the bow kicked against his shoulder, the bolt shooting away from him. It flew up the centre of the stairs and entered the back of the woman's head, blood exploding onto the door in front of her.

For a second, the woman remained upright. Then her legs buckled and she fell backwards. She rolled down the stairs with several clattering thuds before she landed on the larger space of the next floor down with a loud *boom*. The silence that followed seemed to suck all the air from the stairwell.

A second later, the call of two women burst into the area. They came from the first floor rather than the roof. Hopefully the Queen had no idea of any of it.

For a moment, the women paused as they looked at the corpse of their fellow guard. "What the fuck?" one of them said.

Both Flynn and Dan moved around a side of the stairwell each so they were out of sight in the shadows, and out of their path should the women come down. Hopefully they'd come down. If they went to the roof, it would be almost impossible to sneak up on the Queen.

Before the women made any other choice, Flynn freed a buckle from his crossbow harness—it hung down from where he hadn't strapped it around his waist—and he threw it at the door leading in the direction of the foyer. It made a loud *ting!*

The thunder of the two guards' footsteps rushed down towards them.

From his position, Flynn couldn't see Dan, but they both knew what to do. After putting his crossbow down and resting it against the wall, Flynn pulled his machete free and moved alongside the stairs at a crouch, back to where he'd just come from.

The first of the two guards reached the door and grabbed the handle. Before she could pull it open, Flynn and Dan jumped from the shadows at the same time.

Dan buried his knife in the top of one of the guards' heads and Flynn drove his machete through the temple of the other one. Two wet squelches and both guards dropped.

Heavy breaths rocked Flynn's body and he listened for the sounds of more guards. He only heard Dan breathing opposite him. A look up at the top floor and he said, "I need to get my crossbow before we go up there."

After Flynn had retrieved his weapon, he met Dan back at the bottom of the stairs. They didn't speak, but when he led the way, Dan followed behind.

The click of their feet against the metal steps echoed through the hard and cold space. But Flynn also heard the maniacal call of the Queen on the roof. Any small noise they made would have been drowned out by her insane ranting.

At the first floor, Flynn moved to the door leading out into the police station beyond and looked through the small window. It seemed clear. Hopefully the two guards they'd just taken out were the only ones on that floor.

Flynn stepped over the guard he'd shot from the ground and continued up to the roof as soundlessly as possible.

The door leading to the roof had an outline of light from where it hadn't been fully closed. When Flynn reached it and looked through the small gap, he saw two guards standing on the other side. The Queen marched up and down in front of them and they both watched her as she addressed the crowd below.

Yet again, Flynn raised his crossbow, ready to fire. He

stood aside so Dan could peer through the gap. After Dan had pulled away, he nodded. They knew what they had to do.

Another deep breath did little to calm Flynn down. It all rested on this moment, how could he possibly hope for calm? If they took the Queen down, then the people from Home could finish this. An image of Rose in the watery pit ran through his mind and he quickly shook it away. It wouldn't help to think about her at that moment.

Flynn grabbed the metal door handle and counted down in his head.

Three ...
Two ...

CHAPTER 49

One.

Flynn yanked the door open, flooding the corridor with the bright light of the July day. Thankfully the sun shone behind them. They didn't need to be blinded on top of everything else.

Both guards turned around, and before they'd even looked at him, Flynn shot the first one in the temple, blood exploding away from her as the bolt entered one side of her head and exited the other.

A second later, the bolt from Dan's crossbow flew over his shoulder and took the other one out. It too went straight through her head.

No let-up in his pace, Flynn ran across the gravel-covered space and jumped the two collapsing corpses. He rushed at the Queen, the crunch of his footsteps ringing out, the sun on his back.

The vicious woman glanced at Flynn and then shoved the third and final prisoner from the roof. He cried out as he fell, the loud crash of him landing on the trailer cutting his yell short.

Before the Queen had raised her guard, Flynn gave her a hard shove and sent her the same way as the prisoner. Her high-pitched scream rang through the derelict city as the crowd dropped to a new level of silent. Like the man before her, it ended with a loud crash. The usual cheer from the spectators never came.

Heavy breaths ran through Flynn as he walked to the edge of the roof and looked down at the fallen woman. The Queen lay on her back, three glistening spikes puncturing her skinny body. Her dead eyes stared a glassy obsoleteness. Except …

Flynn stepped back, stumbling as if dealt a physical blow. A sea of faces stared up at him from below. They seemed to be waiting for him to say something. Then the people from Home emerged from their hiding places like he'd instructed them to do. He had to speak before they attacked.

"Where is she?" Flynn called out, his shout running through the town as he backed even farther away from the edge of the roof. "Where's the Queen?"

The people of Home stopped. Flynn scanned the crowd. He couldn't see her. "Where are you, you vicious bitch?"

She had to be downstairs. She had to be in the crowd somewhere. Just as Flynn turned around to head back into the building, Dan flew past him. Shoved forwards with a hard thrust, he stumbled, fell, and slid towards the edge of the building. For a second he looked like he'd hold on, his slide over the gravel slowing down. But it didn't slow enough and he toppled out of sight.

Flynn grabbed the handle of his machete, but the Queen moved too quickly for him. She raised her sword so the point of it sat millimetres from his eyeball. The sun glistened off its polished blade.

A look into her cold eyes sent a writhing twist of revulsion through Flynn.

The Queen tilted her head to one side. Tight lips and a vicious scowl, she muttered, "Move and I'll cut your fucking eye out." She smiled. "It looks like you've lost this time, Flynn."

CHAPTER 50

A few metres from the edge of the roof, the Queen motioned for Flynn to move towards it with a flick of her sword. The sun dazzled him as he tried to look at her. He ignored her instruction.

A sneer on her angular face, the Queen said, "You had to come back for that little *slut,* didn't you?" She spoke loud enough for the people in the square to hear her. "Once we had her, we knew you'd be close by. We also knew we just needed to set a trap. And look, you fell for it." A shake of her head. "God, I pity you. Another weak man motivated by his cock. When will you boys learn?"

"I may be a weak man motivated by my cock, yet I wouldn't fuck you, would I?" Flynn said to her.

The Queen pulled her sword away, stepped forward, and threw a backhanded slap across the side of Flynn's face. Light flashed through his vision from the impact, and he tasted his own blood, but he held his ground.

A check over his shoulder into the square, Flynn saw the people from Home put their weapons away and withdraw. Because of the drama on the roof, no one had noticed the near attack from Home. They could still get out of there undetected.

A bitter grin on her sour face, the Queen flicked her sword towards the edge of the roof again.

Flynn remained still.

"You think I'm going to push you off?" the Queen said.

"Of course."

The Queen threw her head back and laughed at the blue sky. While she had her attention on her own glee, Flynn looked at the hunters in the square. Many of them smiled with her.

"Believe me, honey, you'll wish I'd thrown you off the roof by the time I'm done with you. Now we may have lost Mistress, but I can be oh so much crueler than she ever was. I can take you to the edge of death and bring you back again so many times you won't know where you are. You'll question your own mortality, only accepting it because of the excruciating pain that will keep you rooted in reality. I can make it last for years, and believe me, I will."

Nausea clamped Flynn's stomach tight. Panic fluttered through his chest.

When the Queen flicked her sword again, Flynn turned around and moved towards the edge of the roof. Still being careful to hold far enough back, he kept a good metre of gravelly space between him and the fatal drop. He looked at the people of Home. They remained in the crowd. They clearly hadn't given up yet.

"This, ladies and gentlemen," the Queen said, "is what we call a traitor. You're going to see what happens to traitors over the next months and years. He's going to be an example of the consequences of crossing me. I opened the royal complex's doors to him and he betrayed us. He's killed Mistress and all of my royal guards. Who knows who he planned to kill next after me had I not stopped him. Probably all of you. What do you have to say for yourself, traitor?"

When Flynn looked out over the crowd, he noticed movement in the building on his right. Someone shifted through the shadows of the first floor. It took for them to travel through a splash of light for him to recognise who it was. Larry.

The crowd continued to stare up at Flynn, waiting for him to speak.

"Well?" the Queen said and pushed the tip of her sword into his cheek.

The sharp point stung and Flynn drew a short breath. "Notice how we only killed the royal guards." The crowd continued to stare up at him. "If you're not a royal guard, a hunter, or the Queen, you have *nothing* to fear from me."

"What the fuck are you talking about?" The Queen pushed the tip of her sword deeper into the side of his face and Flynn felt a trickle of blood run down his cheek. "You're in no position to make threats."

Another glance to his right and Flynn saw Larry poke his crossbow out of the window. No more than about twenty metres separated him and them. The best aim in Home, if anyone had to make the shot his life depended on, he'd choose Larry.

"Just you wait," Flynn said.

The Queen laughed again, so vigorously she threw her head back and thrust her pelvis forward.

Only an inch, but her laughter had pulled her sword far enough away from Flynn's face. He took his moment and dropped onto the gravelled roof.

The *crack* of a crossbow being fired rang through the square. The bolt landed with a *whomp*.

Flynn looked up to see the hole in the centre of the

Queen's miserable face. Blood belched from the large wound as the vicious bitch's legs buckled, dropping her into a heap.

Flynn jumped to his feet and screamed from the rooftop to the people from Home, "Now!"

They drew their weapons as one and yelled as they closed in on every hunter in the crowd.

CHAPTER 51

It took just minutes for the people from Home to kill every hunter in the square. Maybe some of the crowd were hunters before Home's residents attacked. Maybe they'd dropped their weapons when they understood the situation. But it didn't matter, they'd cut the head off the snake. As long as their loyalty to the Queen had been abandoned with their will to fight, then they had every right to live.

What could have been a volatile and bloody situation hadn't yet erupted. The sun's heat pressed into Flynn's back as he looked out over the crowd, sweat lifting on his brow. They looked nervous, like they worried it could still turn sour for them.

The people of the royal complex outnumbered their counterparts from Home by at least three to one. If they wanted to fight back, they could. But the people from Home were armed, and a war wouldn't end without serious casualties. Flynn had to take control of the situation.

Exhausted and weak from his spent adrenaline and the relief of killing the Queen, Flynn trembled as he lifted her limp form. Fortunately she didn't weigh much. Her feet dragged through the gravel on the roof as he pulled her across to the edge. The collective attention from both sides watched him in silence.

Flynn looked out over a sea of anxious faces and shouted, "Here's your leader." He yelled out from the effort of launching her from the roof and followed her fall most of the way down.

However, by the time she'd connected with the trailer at the bottom—the loud crash exploding through the square—something else had caught his attention. In the chaos of his fight with the Queen, he'd completely forgotten. But now, as he looked down, he nearly lost the strength in his legs. Another skewered body lay on the trailer.

"Dan," Flynn muttered and looked out over the square. In amongst the crowd was one solitary figure. Even with the dense press of bodies, he picked her out instantly. She stood there, frozen in time. She'd already lost her three children and now this. Tears soaked her cheeks.

As they stared at one another, the air left Flynn's lungs in a hard exhale. What could he say to that?

CHAPTER 52

Where chaos had swirled through Flynn's mind, everything now began to settle. Sobered by the sight of Dan on the cart and Sharon's clear grief at the loss of her husband, he then looked at the prisoners also skewered on the medieval device. Even the decoy Queen had died unnecessarily.

Flynn scanned the faces below. Many of them looked pale and scared. Their lives were now in the balance. At least, he wouldn't blame them if they thought that.

When Flynn saw Brian, he found the bearded man staring back at him, like most of the faces below. To ask anything of him took a great effort, the words sticking in his throat. After a cough to clear it, he tried again. "Can you please go and free Rose for me?"

All of the guards and Maggie knew the location of the pit. At present, Flynn couldn't see Maggie in the sea of faces, and Sharon didn't have much in her. Fortunately, Brian nodded at him and exited the square.

The crowd continued to watch Flynn. He looked down at the cart again, the dead people nearly robbing him of his resolve. Then he looked at the Queen. At least one of the bodies deserved to be there. As he lifted his head, he drew a deep breath and pointed down at her. "We did this because she had her sights set on Home. We had to take her and her guards down to alleviate that threat. I've seen what she does to communities, and I couldn't let that happen to anyone else. She had to be stopped, no matter what."

When Flynn paused, silence swept through the square. Every person there listened to his every word.

"We have no beef with the people from the royal complex. Her crazy decisions aren't a reflection of you." Flynn scanned the crowd. "Now, I'm sure there are still hunters in amongst you."

Many in the crowd looked around as if trying to find the people Flynn talked about.

"But we don't care about that. We understand you didn't have a choice in whether you served the Queen or not. I've experienced what she was prepared to do to the people who weren't loyal to her, so I understand your decisions. But you have a choice now. You can make a fresh start. We didn't want to kill anyone, but if you're a threat to us, we'll do what's necessary to end that threat."

A deep breath to steady his nerves, Flynn inhaled the fresh meadowy breeze. His elevated position on the roof allowed him to escape the dusty stink of the town. "The Queen told you she left the bodies of those who died in the games for the people who live in this city."

The crowd remained silent.

"Those people were her and those she kept close, the royal guards and the hunters. The games weren't about giving one person a chance, they were about slaughtering nineteen for the Queen and her mates to get fat on. Although *we* have no beef with the hunters, if there are any left, you might want to keep an eye on them. The likelihood is they've tasted human flesh and might want to again."

If Flynn tried, he'd probably be able to pick out what hunters remained in the crowd from the way the others now looked at them. But he didn't care. They weren't a danger on their own, and from the angry glares thrown at them, they'd be more than punished for their crimes.

"You have a choice how you move forward from here. You have a community that belongs to you now. You have no leader. How you run your community is entirely at your discretion. Just know you have a chance to prosper with that vicious bitch dead. Make the most of it."

Nods moved around the square and the previously tense crowd relaxed a little. They seemed to trust Flynn's words.

"Also, I understand the Queen didn't let anyone have children. You now have a chance to live normal lives. To have families. To work together as a community. You can *serve* one another rather than oppress." Flynn pointed across the rooftops of the town. "We're going back to Home soon. I won't be there, but I'd imagine if you come in peace, there will be trade to be had. We need to move forward as a species. The past twenty years have all been about violence and hostility. We need to give our children something more."

A few people shouted out, making affirmative noises at Flynn.

"We need to be the change we want to see in the world." The words choked him as he thought of Rose and her suffering.

"Good luck," Flynn said to the crowd as an abrupt ending. He turned away from them, jogging across the gravel roof to the door leading back into the police station. On his way, he retrieved his crossbow and machete. He had to get to Rose.

CHAPTER 53

Several dead bodies littered the stairs. Flynn jumped them one at a time as he ran. Whatever happened, he had to get Rose out of that cursed pit. Then he could rest.

The creak of the door's hinges called through the ground floor of the police station. The slap of Flynn's feet echoed through the hallway.

Flynn hit the door leading to the foyer so hard it sent a lightning bolt of pain through his shoulder. The two women he'd killed lay there, along with the one Dan must have dropped on his way in.

A wobble ran through Flynn's legs when he crashed out into the square. It felt like he could fall with every step. But he wouldn't. No fucking way. Not while Rose needed saving.

Fuck knew how the crowd would react to him. To be safe, Flynn kept a hold of his machete. It would be foolish to assume they'd let him pass. Sure, the Queen left little to be desired as a ruler, but he had just toppled a regime the people had grown used to. People resisted change at every step, even positive change.

But the crowd parted for him as he ran through them.

Thank god. After the day he'd had, he didn't want to start slaughtering people who didn't deserve it.

Focused on the wide road leaving the square, Flynn redoubled his efforts and sped up towards it. However, before he reached it, he saw Sharon. He stopped, fighting for breath and sweating as he lifted her hands and stared into her eyes. From the way she looked back at him, glazed and distant, he couldn't be sure if she heard anything he said when he spoke. "I'm so sorry."

No flash of recognition, Sharon nodded all the same.

Several more of Home's residents stood close to Sharon. Flynn thanked them all. They'd been brave; they needed recognition of that. When he saw Larry, he put a hand on his shoulder and said, "Thank you."

Although Larry nodded, he frowned like he had something on his mind. When he stepped aside, Flynn saw what.

The dead body of a girl lay on her back. Someone had taken their sweatshirt off and draped it across her face.

Dread sank through Flynn's gut to look at the body. A shake of his head and he said, "No, not another one." He knew before they pulled the shirt away, but he continued to shake his head as if the action would somehow falsify the reality in front of him. It didn't.

Blood covered her young face. A compassionate girl with a big heart, death had turned her ugly. Her frozen look of horror forced Flynn back a step. A blurred view of her through his tears and his voice wobbled as he said, "Dear Maggie, not you too."

CHAPTER 54

To look at the dead Maggie dragged Flynn back to the moment he'd killed Serj. Already exhausted, he lost a little more strength. Serj had always touted Maggie as Home's next leader. Although he hadn't voiced it, it seemed like he wanted to wait until she was old enough before he handed responsibility of the place over to her. He'd called her a bright spark, the future of Home. Someone who'd be able to stand up to the bullshit of Brian, Sharon, and Dan. Although, to look at Sharon now made it hard to believe there would be any more bullshit from her. She might never come back from Dan's death.

After a deep sigh, Flynn shook his head. As much as he wanted to help, he couldn't do anything for the girl now. Maggie had gone and Rose still needed him. As crass as it seemed, he turned from the grieving group of Home's residents and ran off down the wide road leading to the plaza with the pit in it.

Everyone remained in the square, so Flynn moved down the road on his own. How would it impact Home's residents to be minus two of their most influential people? Who would lead them out of it? Could they trust Brian to do the right thing? Did he have it in him? And what about the future? While Maggie lived, Serj had always had hope for the place. Had the hope just died with her?

Flynn couldn't think about any of it. As much as Home had been a part of his life, it wouldn't be for much longer. After he'd freed Rose from that cursed pit, he'd be leaving the place for good.

∽

As Flynn ran from the alleyway alongside the hotel into the wide-open plaza, he stumbled and almost tripped at what he saw. The cage lay open, the metal grate flat against the ground from where it had been pulled wide. Brian stood over it, staring into the murky water.

"Brian!" Flynn called as he ran towards him.

Brian didn't look up.

"Brian!" Flynn called again. "Where are they?"

Still, the man continued to stare into the filthy pool.

Another stumble, but Flynn pushed on. When he got next to Brian, he fought to get his breaths back. The reek of stagnation ran up his nostrils, the muddy tang stimulating his gag reflex. No doubt many bodies had rotted at the bottom of the watery pit. Not that he could see through the muddy churn of it. "Where are they?"

Brian shook his head and continued to stare into the water. In no more than a whisper, he said, "I don't know. I found the pit like this."

What little strength Flynn had been holding onto left him. Unable to stop it, his legs folded beneath him and he landed in a heap.

CHAPTER 55

Aches sat deep in Flynn's body. They ran from his toes to the end of the hairs on his head. Every time he shifted slightly, lightning bolts of pain lit him up. His arse hurt more than anything from where he'd sat on the hard stone ground in the plaza for what felt like days, but in reality, it might not have been any more than two or three hours.

The sun had nearly set, casting shadows through the town. Much longer and it would be as dark in the plaza as the stinking water in front of him. The fading light made the pit seem more ominous than before, like it went down for miles. How far would they have to dive if they wanted to retrieve Rose's body?

"You can't stay here forever."

Flynn turned to look at the alleyway leading out of the plaza. Brian had been gone for some time, but he now stood there with his arm around Sharon. Pale faced with red, puffy eyes, tears still streamed down her cheeks as she looked at him.

"We need to get you back to Home," Brian said. "We've buried Dan and Maggie. Everyone else has already left."

"I'm going to wait," Flynn called back.

"You can't. It's getting dark."

Flynn shouted this time, his voice echoing through the square. "I'm going to wait!"

"For what?" Sharon said. "Nomads? We've lost too many good people already, Flynn."

The footsteps of Brian and Sharon bounced off the walls of the plaza as they moved close to Flynn, and Sharon spoke in a softer voice. "We're all hurting. But if Rose had made it, she'd be here by now."

"Shut up!" Flynn shouted. He jumped to his feet and pointed at Sharon. "How do *you* know she's gone?"

Washed out with grief, Sharon let go of a deep sigh. "We've all lost someone, Flynn."

Sharon's calmness completely disarmed him. She wore her grief unmasked and stared it straight at him.

Tears burned in Flynn's eyes and his view of Home's two guards blurred. His face buckled.

Sharon closed the distance between them. She wrapped him in a tight hug and cried with him. "I know it hurts," she said between sobs. "Believe me, I know."

CHAPTER 56

Nausea balled in Flynn's stomach, twisting tighter every time he looked at his breakfast of unleavened bread, tomatoes, and goat's milk cheese. As much as he wanted to eat, he couldn't. Sure, many people would kill in this new world to have a plate of fresh food in front of them, but as he sat outside Home—the sun rising on a new day—he couldn't eat a thing.

Sharon and Brian both sat with him at a long bench, but neither of them spoke. What could they say? They'd lost too much. Words just didn't cut it anymore.

When Angelica walked over, tension coiled in Flynn and his shoulders wound tight. He turned away from her.

Faux friendliness, sickly sweet in its disingenuousness, she said, "Can I sit with you guys?"

Aware of Sharon and Brian nodding, Flynn balled his fists and fought to keep his breaths even. He knew exactly what she was doing and he wanted no fucking part of it.

The bench shifted when she sat down on it. As she moved close to him, he caught the smell of flowers on her. Something she used to do when they were together in their early days.

"I just wanted to thank you for saving Home," Angelica said. "To thank all of you. Especially you, Flynn."

The touch of Angelica's hand against his forearm made Flynn flinch and he pulled away from her. A hard glare and he spoke through gritted teeth. "Don't touch me."

"Don't be like that."

A look across the line of tables and Flynn saw Larry at one close by. A voice loud enough so he could hear, he said, "You want to find a hero, you should look to the guy you're fucking. Were it not for him, I'd be dead by now and the Queen would have won. Maybe, rather than picking the person who suits you best at the time, you should focus on who you're with. Otherwise you're going to end up miserable and alone."

Angelica opened her mouth to reply, but Flynn cut her off. "Stop being a cunt. It's simple."

Tears gathered in Angelica's eyes and she got to her feet. Her lip bent out of shape for a moment and then fury twisted her features as she spat, "I just wanted to say *thanks*."

A sneer and Flynn shook his head at her. "It's never as simple as that with you. You *always* want something."

Angelica pressed her lips tightly together, her body rocking with her quick breaths. "I'm going to guard the gate," she then said to Brian and Sharon. Neither said anything; instead they both nodded at her.

As she walked off, Flynn returned his attention to his untouched breakfast. Hopefully he'd find the stomach to eat it soon. Good meals shouldn't ever go to waste.

CHAPTER 57

Fuck knew how long had passed. The sun had grown hotter as the day moved on and it now sat in the sky directly above Flynn. The heat of it soaked into his tired muscles and kept him rooted to the spot.

Flynn had stared at his breakfast for the entire time. Still unable to touch it, his eyes stung from exhaustion and they threatened to close every few seconds, but he couldn't give over to sleep. As much as he wanted to, his overactive mind wouldn't let him.

Sharon had offered Flynn lunch about an hour ago. How she'd managed to keep going with the loss of Dan, he didn't know. He politely declined and continued to remain in the same spot.

Most of Home rested that day. It had been quiet the entire time, and even when the little kids played, their parents took them far away so their noise didn't disturb anyone. So when Angelica raised her voice on the gate, it carried over the stillness.

"You're not welcome here."

Flynn looked over at her and saw the anger in her tense body. She stood guard on her own.

"Why don't you just fuck off?" Angelica said.

Maybe she thought no one could hear her. When she raised one of the gate's crossbows, Flynn got to his feet. "Who are you talking to, Angelica?"

But she ignored him, her hands shaking as she pointed her bow down.

Dread dropped through Flynn. Something didn't add up. "Angelica? What are you doing?"

Flynn could see she'd heard him because she tensed up at his words, but she still didn't reply. He stepped away from the bench and ran over to her. "Angelica!"

"She's no good for you, Flynn."

"What the fuck are you talking about?"

"She's done nothing but cause you trouble. She got you involved with the Queen. She brought the war down on us."

Flynn's heart beat like a bass drum. "Angelica, put the crossbow down."

Clearly not caring who heard her now, Angelica screamed, "No!" She looked down the barrel of her crossbow and shouted, "She's bad news. I'm not letting her in."

Not that he needed to hear it to know who waited on the other side of the gate, but when Rose said, "Please, just let me see him," his heart damn near stopped.

CHAPTER 58

Flynn looked at how impossibly far away Angelica stood at that moment. At any point, she could pull the trigger and Rose would die.

Suddenly something flashed through the air above him and Angelica screamed.

Blood exploded from the top of her left arm and she dropped the crossbow. The weapon spun through the air as it fell several feet to the ground. When it crashed against the dusty track, it jolted as it released its bolt. Fortunately it fired straight into one of the thick wooden gates, sticking into the hard wood.

A look behind him and Flynn saw Larry standing there with his crossbow still raised.

Larry looked at Flynn too. They stood frozen for a few seconds.

Then Flynn burst to life, running the last few steps to the gate. He undid the bolts with three loud snaps and pulled the right gate wide open.

Crying as he said it, Flynn gasped, "Rose?"

Rose stepped forward, threw her arms wide, and wrapped Flynn in a tight hug.

Flynn squeezed back like he'd never let go of her again. "My god, am I pleased to see you. I thought I'd lost you."

When they finally pulled away from one another, Rose smiled. "We've just gotta have faith it'll work out, right?" She then leaned forward and kissed him, pressing her lips so hard against his it almost hurt.

CHAPTER 59

"We've locked her in a cell," Larry said as he sat down at one of the tables outside the main building. Flynn, Rose, Brian, Sharon, and several more people from Home were already sitting there.

"Thank you," Flynn said to him. "Not that I wanted to see it come to this. I'm sorry it played out like it did."

Larry shook his head. "It's not your fault. Angelica chose to act in that way. You can only be an arsehole for so long in such a small community before you get found out."

"So?" Sharon said, looking at Rose as she turned her palms to the sky. "What happened?"

Halfway through a mouthful of stew, Rose quickly chewed and swallowed it down. She even looked beautiful when she ate. Even more beautiful considering Flynn had almost written her off. She pulled her blonde hair away from her face and smiled. "I found a way out of the pit. When we were in there, I found a tunnel and tried swimming down it. I went down and came back several times, going a little bit farther every time." She screwed her face up. "The water was disgusting. I had to get to the end of my breath and I thought my lungs would burst, but I eventually found a manhole cover, which came free. Once I was out, I opened the cage and freed the rest of the women. It was a good job it was all kicking off in the square. It gave us the cover to get out of there."

"And what happened to the others?" Flynn said. "What about the pregnant woman? Was she okay?"

"They were *all* pregnant, Flynn."

Several of the people at the bench gasped.

"The Queen put anyone who got pregnant into the pit to be eaten. She didn't want to be reminded of her infertility. Also, she believed that if she ate pregnant women and their babies, maybe she'd become fertile."

"What the fuck?" Flynn said. He looked at his stew and then pushed it away from him.

"I know." Rose's eyes opened wide. "Mental, right?"

"So what's happened to the women?"

"I took them back to the royal complex. With the Queen gone, they decided they wanted to stay there. Many of them still had partners there."

"The Queen only took the women?"

"Yeah."

"And the men did nothing about it?"

"It would seem not. I mean, what could they do against her rule? And maybe they didn't know where they'd gone."

"I suppose. And the woman who lost her partner?"

"She wanted to stay with them. There were seven women in total and they wanted to go through childbirth together."

Brian spoke this time, his face red, almost as if he felt embarrassed to say it. "You know you two can stay here, right? For as long as you like."

When Rose looked at Flynn, he shook his head. "No, we can't. Thank you for the offer, but I have too much history here. Besides, you can't keep Angelica locked up forever, and I'm not sure I want to be in a place where she is."

A tilt of his head to one side, Brian said, "The offer will always be here. This is your home. A lot of shit's gone on over the years and we may not have seen eye to eye, but you're a stand-up guy and an asset to any community."

Rose reached across and held Flynn's hand.

"Whatever's happened before now," Brian continued, "I'd like to wipe the slate clean." He held his hand out in Flynn's direction.

The attention of everyone burned into Flynn and his face heated from the focus of them all. The gentle reassurance from Rose's warm grip helped him push on. A dip of his head and he shook Brian's hand. "I appreciate that. And I wish you all the best for Home moving forward."

Several people around the table smiled. Sharon didn't. It would be a long time before she smiled again.

CHAPTER 60

They'd said their goodbyes and walked away from Home through the long grass. They had half a day of light still ahead of them.

Since Rose had come back, Flynn couldn't stop looking at her. He'd come so close to losing her. They held hands as they walked, the sound of the wind flying over the landscape.

Before Flynn could speak, he heard something behind them. The snapping of a twig. The rustle of grass. He dropped Rose's hand and spun around with his crossbow raised, his pulse thudding.

What he saw took his breath away.

Rose spoke first in no more than a whisper. "A white hart."

Flynn lowered his bow and smiled as he stared at the creature. As white as snow, it stood out from a mile away in its lush green surroundings. Then it snapped its head in his direction and stared at him for a second before it turned around and ran.

"How do you think it's survived for as long as it has? I mean, standing out like it does," Rose said.

"Maybe no one has it in them to kill something so beautiful," Flynn said, watching the creature disappear from his view. He reattached his crossbow and reached out for Rose's hand again.

The meadow stretched out in front of them as they walked in a direction Flynn hadn't yet walked in. In all the time he'd been in Home, they'd stuck to familiar paths. It had always been enough. But now they wanted to go somewhere different.

"So where are we going?" Rose said as she looked across at Flynn, the wind tossing her long blonde hair.

A shrug and Flynn smiled. "Wherever fate takes us."

THE END.

∾

Thank you for reading The Alpha Plague 8.

If you'd like to try any more of my work, I have another series called The Shadow Order. Book 1 is available for FREE. Find it at www.michaelrobertson.co.uk

MICHAEL ROBERTSON

THE SHADOW ORDER

A SPACE OPERA

∼

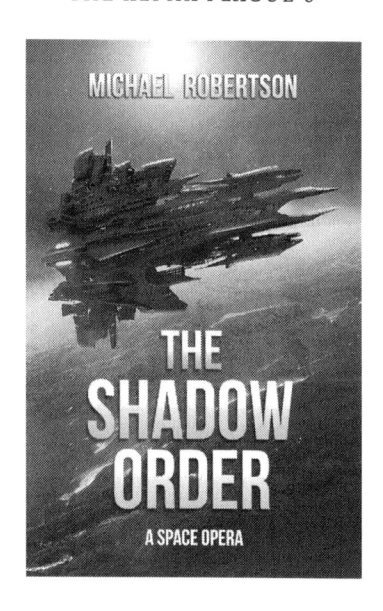

Would you like to be notified of all my future releases and special offers? Join my spam-free mailing list for all of my updates at www.michaelrobertson.co.uk

∼

Support the Author

DEAR READER, AS AN INDEPENDENT AUTHOR I DON'T HAVE the resources of a huge publisher. If you like my work and would like to see more from me in the future, there are two things you can do to help: leaving a review, and a word-of-mouth referral.

Releasing a book takes many hours and hundreds of dollars. I love to write, and would love to continue to do so.

All I ask is that you leave an Amazon review. It shows other readers that you've enjoyed the book and will encourage them to give it a try too. The review can be just one sentence, or as long as you like.

∼

If you've enjoyed The Alpha Plague and The Shadow Order, you may also enjoy my post-apocalyptic series - Crash (please be warned, this is a very dark series, and not to everyone's liking) - Book 1 is FREE:

Find Crash at www.michaelrobertson.co.uk

ABOUT THE AUTHOR

Like most children born in the seventies, Michael grew up with Star Wars in his life. An obsessive watcher of the films, and an avid reader from an early age, he found himself taken over with stories whenever he let his mind wander.

Those stories had to come out.

He hopes you enjoy reading his books as much as he does writing them.

Michael loves to travel when he can. He has a young family, who are his world, and when he's not reading, he enjoys walking so he can dream up more stories.

Contact

www.michaelrobertson.co.uk
subscribers@michaelrobertson.co.uk

ALSO BY MICHAEL ROBERTSON

The Shadow Order

The First Mission - Book Two of The Shadow Order

The Crimson War - Book Three of The Shadow Order

Eradication - Book Four of The Shadow Order

120-Seconds: A Shadow Order Story

∿

The Alpha Plague: A Post-Apocalyptic Action Thriller

The Alpha Plague 2

The Alpha Plague 3

The Alpha Plague 4

The Alpha Plague 5

The Alpha Plague 6

The Alpha Plague 7

The Alpha Plague 8

∿

Crash - A Dark Post-Apocalyptic Tale

Crash II: Highrise Hell

Crash III: There's No Place Like Home

Crash IV: Run Free

Crash V: The Final Showdown

New Reality: Truth

New Reality 2: Justice

New Reality 3: Fear

OTHER AUTHORS UNDER THE SHEILD
OF PHALANX PRESS

Sixth Cycle

Nuclear war has destroyed human civilization.
Captain Jake Phillips wakes into a dangerous new world, where he finds the remaining fragments of the population living in a series of strongholds, connected across the country. Uneasy alliances have maintained their safety, but things are about to change. -- Discovery **leads to danger.** -- Skye Reed, a tracker from the Omega stronghold, uncovers a threat that could spell the end for their fragile society. With friends and enemies revealing truths about the past, she will need to decide who to trust. -- Sixth **Cycle** is a gritty post-apocalyptic story of survival and adventure.

Darren Wearmouth ~ Carl Sinclair

~

DEAD ISLAND: Operation Zulu

Ten years after the world was nearly brought to its knees by a zombie Armageddon, there is a race for the antidote! On a remote Caribbean island, surrounded by a horde of hungry living dead, a team of American and Australian commandos must rescue the Antidotes' scientist. Filled with zombies, guns, Russian bad guys, shady government types, serial killers and elevator muzak. Dead Island is an action packed blood soaked horror adventure.

Allen Gamboa

Invasion Of The Dead Series

This is the first book in a series of nine, about an ordinary bunch of friends, and their plight to survive an apocalypse in Australia. -- Deep beneath defense headquarters in the Australian Capital Territory, the last ranking Army chief and a brilliant scientist struggle with answers to the collapse of the world, and the aftermath of an unprecedented virus. Is it a natural mutation, or does the infection contain -- more sinister roots? -- One hundred and fifty miles away, five friends returning from a month-long camping trip slowly discover that death has swept through the country. What greets them in a gradual revelation is an enemy beyond compare. -- Armed with dwindling ammunition, the friends must overcome their disagreements, utilize their individual skills, and face unimaginable horrors as they battle to reach their hometown...

Owen Ballie

Whiskey Tango Foxtrot

Alone in a foreign land. The radio goes quiet while on convoy in Afghanistan, a lost patrol alone in the desert. With his unit and his home base destroyed, Staff Sergeant Brad Thompson suddenly finds himself isolated and in command of a small group of men trying to survive in the Afghan wasteland. **Every turn leads to danger**

The local population has been afflicted with an illness that turns them into rabid animals. They pursue him and his men at every corner and stop. Struggling to hold his team together and unite survivors, he must fight and evade his way to safety. **A fast paced zombie war story like no other.**

W.J. Lundy

∽

Zombie Rush

New to the Hot Springs PD Lisa Reynolds was not all that welcomed by her coworkers especially those who were passed over for the position. It didn't matter, her thirty days probation ended on the same day of the Z-poc's arrival. Overnight the world goes from bad to worse as thousands die in the initial onslaught. National Guard and regular military unit deployed the day before to the north leaves the city in mayhem. All directions lead to death until one unlikely candidate steps forward with a plan. A plan that became an avalanche raging down the mountain culminating in the salvation or destruction of them all.

Joseph Hansen

∽

The Gathering Horde

The most ambitious terrorist plot ever undertaken is about to be put into motion, releasing an unstoppable force against humanity. Ordinary people – A group of students celebrating the end of the semester, suburban and rural families – are about to themselves in the center of something that threatens the survival of the human species. As they battle the dead – and the living – it's going to take every bit of skill, knowledge and luck for them to survive in Zed's World.

Rich Baker

Printed in Great Britain
by Amazon